THORNWOOD ACADEMY 2:
DEAD TO ME

LJ SWALLOW

Chapter One

VIOLET

"The blood is mine."

I stare blankly at Grayson as he wipes at his face with a damp, dark blue towel. Not the explanation I expected. "The blood? On your face?"

"Is my blood. Yes."

There're two disturbing issues here.

Firstly, why?

Secondly, I'm attracted to that blood. *His* blood. Well, I guess you missed an ingredient in your potion, Mother. Sure, I couldn't differentiate vamp blood by smell, but I sure as hell liked the taste. And now I've tasted, I can scent that variety.

Or just Grayson's? Crap.

"Oh." My hands dangle uselessly by my sides as I remain by the door leading out of his room. I'm certainly notching up my academy rule-breaking tonight: two guys' rooms in one evening. Unlike Rowan's chaos, Grayson's is immaculate, as if staged for an academy brochure as one of Thornwood's premier rooms. I'm increasingly annoyed that my father never arranged one for me.

He frowns. "Is that explanation enough for you?" I shake my head. "Why are you quiet? It makes me nervous."

"Uh. I've never seen a vampire covered in their own blood." Obviously, otherwise I might've engaged in some face-licking.

Good grief, Violet.

Grayson mistakes my pained expression for something else. "Don't worry. I'm not hurt anymore."

"Anymore?" I wrap my arms around myself, debating the sense in staying in Grayson's room. But I did demand an explanation and I agreed to speak to him alone.

I smelled Grayson's blood. I tasted his blood. Now I've seen him in the light, I can tell this is vamp—it's darker and thicker like mine, something I couldn't see both times I encountered Grayson in the dark.

"What happened? Did you fight? Or did the people you killed fight back?"

Grayson goes deadly still. Is he about to strike? "I did not kill," he snaps. "And if I did, wouldn't I have shifter blood on me right now?" I recoil as he holds out the towel. "Smell."

My eyes widen. "I'd rather not."

"Don't panic, it's vamp blood. That won't tempt you." He waves the navy towel. Sensible color choice—less persistent blood stains.

"I believe you," I shoot back.

This is bad. Very, very bad.

"Or is my blood tempting you?" His lips twitch into a smile. "Violet?"

"Certainly not," I retort, perhaps a little too quickly.

"You're freaked out by something," he says and drops the towel onto his bed.

"Yes. Like you said, another body, another Blackwood

rune." I swallow. He's wearing a partially buttoned black shirt, but I can smell the blood on that too.

"Violet?" I blink up at him. "Normally you gaze into my eyes, not at my chest."

"I do not gaze into your eyes."

"'Kay." Grayson grabs the shirt by one shoulder and pulls it over his head before dumping it next to the towel on his perfectly made bed.

"Is this a weird mating display, Grayson?" I ask, now presented with his naked torso. "Because if you're about to strip in front of me, don't."

"Otherwise, you'll leave?"

"No, otherwise the response you get will be painful and not the one you're looking for."

"And there she is." Grayson grins and grabs a clean black T-shirt from a drawer, the scent of detergent at last obscuring his own. "So, what should we talk about first?"

We remain standing and I'm ready to bolt if he comes any closer. I need to speak to Eloise. Some daughters might approach their mother to discuss 'confusing feelings about boys', but this is next level.

"I'm glad you healed quickly," I say truthfully. "What hurt you?"

"The people I met." He moistens his lips.

"If they hurt you the first night, when Wesley died, why meet these people again?"

"'These people' often hurt me." Grayson moves to sit on the bed and kicks off his boots. "That wasn't the first time."

"Right. And that's acceptable to you?" I pause. "You like their treatment? Because you don't seem particularly concerned."

"It's complicated."

I sigh. "Why is that always people's answer to awkward questions? If you don't want to tell me, just say so."

"Oh, I'll tell you the whole story some time, but right now

I just need you to believe the blood isn't Rory's and I haven't killed."

"I can unequivocally say I believe that is your blood." A thought hits. The night Wesley died, that's why I obsessively followed the trail—it was *Grayson's* blood.

"Did anybody see you in town or the woods tonight, Violet?" Grayson pushes long fingers through his hair. "Where were you before I found you?"

"With Rowan."

"Where?"

"In his room."

"Doing what?" He shakes his head. "Or don't I want to know?"

"You'd be upset if you knew what I did with Rowan." *Do not tune into emotions again.* "I don't want to talk about what happened."

Grayson hisses and jumps up. "Did Rowan assault you? I'll fucking kill him."

Good grief. "Grayson. When persuading someone you're not a murderer, such a statement does not help." He looks around with halfway to black vamp eyes, his features altering too. "And put that face away. Rowan wouldn't and couldn't hurt me."

"And how can you be so sure? What if he's the killer?" he growls.

"If by any chance he is, I'm still certain Rowan won't hurt me."

"I suppose... Trying to murder you wouldn't be a sensible move if Rowan wanted to stay intact." His stance slackens. "But something's happened. Your energy's weird."

"I joined magic with Rowan to help his psychometry."

"Huh." Grayson snatches his dirty shirt and tosses it into a basket beside his desk, the unwanted blood scent drifting my way again. "The spell he used to claim I killed Wesley? And what was that crap you said to me about coats?"

I scoot over to sit on his desk chair, ready to fight any emerging bloodlust from a distance in order to find answers. "Do you and Rowan get along?"

"We're not friends, but we're not enemies. He has a weird vibe."

Does everybody get classified by 'vibes' in this world? What are these intangible things? "Has he accused you of something?" I continue.

Grayson swings his legs so he's lying on the bed, fingers locked behind his head, pulling up his T-shirt. I snap my head up before he accuses me of staring at his vampiric physique again.

"If Rowan did accuse me to my face, he'd do so to help you, Violet. The guy's *weird* about you." *And he'll be weirder now.* "I reckon Rowan thinks I'll draw you into the 'ways of the hemia'," he says, playing up his words with a dramatic tone. "Awaken your bloodlust."

Blood rushes to my cheeks and I pray that in the dim he can't see them. How will I ever spend time around this guy in the future and remain distant?

"I have a potion for that," I say. "I've no desire or stomach for blood."

Grayson abruptly sits. "A potion that suppresses your blood lust?"

"That's what I said."

"How? Where from?" he asks sharply, and I'm taken aback at his sudden, intense change in demeanor.

"I'm only half-vamp. That's probably why a potion works. I can't see how anything would help a full hemia like you."

He snorts and lies back down, staring at the ceiling. "Judgmental, much? You might change when you're older."

"Won't."

"Blood taking is about more than feeding, Violet," he says and turns his head towards me. "You know that."

I stand abruptly at his words. "I should go."

I can't allow Grayson to detect there's a new weakness, specifically towards him, that'll sway my desire for blood. With this and the witch bond causing stability issues with Rowan, I definitely need to speak to my mother.

Especially since another murder occurred tonight.

"Oh, shit!" Grayson sits up and swings his legs round. "Is that the problem? Witch blood? Did you and Rowan indulge, and things got awkward?"

I gawk at him. "I don't drink blood. It repulses me." But *his*? I swallow. "No. The only thing Rowan and I shared is magic and after performing the spell we argued, and I left."

"Yeah, I can see how you'd clash. Were you with him all evening?"

"I left Holly around eight. What time did you find me in the woods?"

"Shrieking like a banshee? Around nine."

"I didn't leave Rowan much before then, so I have an alibi." I brighten for the first time, although Rowan may not find that news as shiny.

"I don't." Grayson taps his lips. "And I have your boyfriend pointing fingers at me for one death already."

"Rowan isn't my boyfriend."

"He's something. You're too alike."

My jaw clenches tight. Yes, he's something alright. Grayson swayed the conversation. Smart. But I've more questions and he's basically trapped in this room with me.

"If you won't tell me the story why you were covered in your own blood, tell me if you approached Wesley's body. Did Rowan see that, or was he tricking me?"

Grayson studies me silently for a moment. "Okay. On my way back to the academy, I saw someone on the ground and stopped to see if the person was okay. I could smell the blood before I reached Wes but didn't know who it was. Maybe that's why Rowan saw me in his spell?" He drags a hand through his hair. "I would've helped, Violet, but as soon as I

6

knew for certain the guy was dead, I ran. If anybody found me near Wes's body, they'd accuse me."

"Did you see him clearly? The rune?" Grayson nods. "Why didn't you tell anybody, Grayson?"

"Wesley was dead, Violet."

"But still, you left him..." I trail off as his eyes widen. "As a Blackwood, I understand why you did nothing."

He looks at me. "Do you? Because others might not."

"I presume you were questioned after the murder."

"Yeah, but the witches didn't get through to my memories between leaving and returning to campus." He pauses. "Or of meeting you."

I straighten. "Do you think I killed Wesley?"

"No! You wouldn't leave his body where someone could find him. And you're too disconnected from everything to care."

"And Rory's body?"

He chews his lip. "This time, I saw two guys in the woods from a distance. Which isn't unusual because people often take a shortcut through there, but I worried they'd see me and the blood." He wipes at where his face was stained. "I ran before they'd gotten close enough for me to scent *what* the guys were, because if they were shifters, they'd know there was a vamp around."

"Did you touch Rory?"

"I tripped over him." He shakes his head. "So, yeah. We're both on this body. Your rune and me."

"You tripped?" I ask in horror. "You're a vampire. What happened to your reflexes?"

"Someone screamed, Violet." He looks at me pointedly. "Distracted me, and I didn't see the body as I ran."

This gets worse for both of us.

"What's wrong? Don't you believe me?" He scowls. "Look in my mind if you want."

"You're right—there's no shifter blood on you. I can only

scent yours. The two guys you saw—they had something to do with Rory's death."

"Maybe Kai?" he suggests. "His gang obviously has beef with the shifters."

"But why would Kai kill Wesley too?" I shake my head. "If you're telling me there's a rune on Rory's body, the same person killed both."

Grayson shrugs. "How do we know that Kai didn't have a motive to kill Wes? I hope he becomes a suspect too. Focusing only on supes isn't fair."

I make a derisive noise. "I doubt Kai will be arrested. *I'll* be the accused again—and you, if you've left any kind of imprint on the body."

"So, what do we do?" he asks.

Do? Something practical and necessary. "We keep away from each other."

"Why?" He frowns.

"Several reasons, including association with a girl suspected of two murders could be unwise for you." I compose myself and stand. "Thank you for your help this evening and for telling me what I believe is the truth. Although why you didn't just tell me before—"

"You might've told someone."

My eyes go wide. "What?"

"Well, you're only bothered about yourself, and handing me over to authorities would help your cause."

"And cause a lot of trouble for you?" My lips thin. "Just because I don't care for people doesn't mean I support injustice. I wouldn't want you falsely accused."

He crosses his arms. "Why?"

"You're Petrescu. As a Blackwood, I understand that your name would be considered before any other evidence."

"Yeah. Those bloody names."

"I'm happy to be the last Blackwood. I'm just *unhappy* that my name probably made me a target." I sigh. "I thought this murder would be simple to figure out, but now I'm growing rather frustrated."

"Now the murders are about you, not Wesley. Or Rory." Grayson pulls a sympathetic face. "Someone's framing you, Violet."

"Mmm." I step back in alarm as he grabs his damp towel and approaches me, bringing temptation with him. "What are you doing?"

"When you bit me, you drew blood and you've some on your face. You definitely can't walk through campus like that."

"Fine, I—" Grayson wipes my cheek and as he touches the other to hold my face, he becomes a victim of my reflexes. In seconds, he's slammed across the room, hitting his head on the side of the desk.

"What the fuck, Violet?"

"Don't!"

"That was an overreaction!" He touches the side of his head and I smell the blood smeared on his fingers before I see the dark red, and the same blinding rush of bloodlust rears its head.

"Sorry. I need to go. Thank you again for your help."

I'm out of that door in a heartbeat.

Chapter Two

VIOLET

I SLEEP BADLY.

Normally I sleep little anyway, but since arriving at Thornwood every day leaves me exhausted. This morning I woke up feeling as if I've died and somebody reanimated me badly, my brain and body sluggish.

The room already fills with Holly's favorite perfume of the week, the floral notes less overpowering than usual, which means she's left.

I squint at the phone. 7am. My first thought: does anybody know about the second murder yet? When will somebody report Rory missing? I debated informing someone last night, but Grayson is correct about distancing ourselves as much as possible. Violet Blackwood reporting a murder? Not sensible.

Class starts in an hour; I'll follow routine until the inevitable happens and I'm hauled over the coals again.

I send a message to Eloise.

I need your help, tell D you both need to come
to Thornwood

As I lay my uniform on the bed, I glance over at the phone a few times, but Eloise doesn't respond. I shower and dress but discover one crucial element in my morning routine is missing. Holly keeps a plethora of tiny bottles and packets of pain medication in the small cabinet beneath the sink, and I place my 'tonic' in the same place. After Rowan's invasion, I decanted the pink potion into one of Holly's cleaned bottles, and then hid it amongst Holly's things.

This morning—no bottle.

An unwanted and recently acquired response smacks me in the chest—panic. Pulling every bottle and box from the cupboard until they're strewn around me on the floor, I carefully check each one, heart thumping in my ears.

No.

No, no, *no*.

The room door opens and closes and through the bathroom entrance, I see Holly in uniform, hair scraped back from her face, walk towards her bed. She pauses as she sees me kneeling on the floor.

"Violet? What's wrong?" Holly peruses my black sweats and tank top I wear to bed. "Why aren't you dressed yet?"

"Did you take anything from here?" I ask and point at the cupboard, keeping my voice steady. "My tonic."

I haven't told Holly exactly what the potion is or does, although she regarded me with suspicion and replied, "I won't ask" when I produced the concoction from my trunk.

Holly's the only person who knows I keep the potion in this cupboard.

"No." Holly walks across and looks down. "Are you alright? You arrived back late last night." I gather up her things to tuck them back in the cupboard. Did I leave the potion elsewhere? "Busy night with Rowan, huh?" she teases.

Rowan. My chest tightens again. I'd pushed him to the back of my mind, intending to avoid him, but that's now impossible.

Rowan's my alibi.

Or if he's unlucky, a joint suspect.

Did anybody see or hear us last night? Rowan's room is at the far end of Pendle House, but somebody must've heard me yelling at him.

"Violet?" I blink out of my thoughts. "Did something bad happen?"

"I need my tonic. It's important. Were you here *all* last night?" She nods. But I only take this once a day—whoever stole the bottle could've walked in during the daytime.

Someone at the academy with a key and who knows about the potion.

Who? Until I told Grayson last night, the potion was a secret between me and my family. Grayson didn't have time— I returned straight here after my hasty departure.

I swear and stand, shoving my hands into my pants pockets. How long before the potion's effects wear off? Will somebody need to bleed near me, or will everybody have the effect Grayson does?

"I can't go to class today," I inform Holly.

"Don't you feel well? Is that why you need your tonic?" Her face softens with concern, which is preferable to suspicion at this point. "Maybe the nurse has some spare if it's a common supe thing?"

"She won't." I take a shuddery breath. "What class do we have first?"

"Art. Should I tell Ms. Reynolds that you're unwell?"

I nod, already holding my breath. The longest I've gone between doses is twenty-four hours. I could be lucky—the potion's magic might not disappear straightaway.

But Rowan? Witch blood. What if my meeting with him

12

ends in disaster? Because he's the person I need to see right now, and if the vampire wakes, witch blood will become irresistible. And my bonded witch's blood? I don't want to imagine what I might do to him.

Chapter Three

VIOLET

I've no reply from Eloise even with my follow up text telling her that I need help because my potion 'spilled'. If the potions effects might wear off, I need to get to Rowan quickly. He answers my text straightaway, agreeing to meet me.

I insist on outside—I need open space with plenty of fresh air around. Rowan waits for me at the edge of campus where the chain fence meets the entrance to the woods. I pause a good few meters away from where Rowan's standing close to a thick-trunked tree. He's adopted his more guarded stance and frankly I can't blame him.

Will the bond change my physical response to him on other levels? Rowan isn't unpleasant to look at—like much of the so-called witch royalty, he has a strong jawline and heavy brow, full lips that once permanently smirked at me and despite his often 'dragged through a hedge' couture, there's an unusual attractiveness to him.

Not to me, obviously, but I've heard whispers from girls who'd like to catch his attention due to his attractive traits. At the high school, I witnessed girls chasing 'the mysterious loner' many times. Does Rowan ever take advantage of such opportunities?

"Are you leaving?" he asks curtly and gestures at my lack of uniform. "Is this a goodbye moment?"

"I can't leave. Not yet."

"Then why, sweet Violet, did you ask to see me? You never wanted me to breathe in your direction again." I push my tongue against my teeth at his snark. So, we're back to normal in one respect—let's hope that continues. "And less than a day later, you want to meet up." He digs hands into his trouser pockets. "What's happening?"

Even if we don't mention the bond, it's around us, our mingled magic energies tangibly stronger in each other's presence. "I'm sure you find my presence as difficult as I find yours, Rowan."

"For many reasons," he says, tone harsh. "Answer the question."

The breeze from the early spring day ruffles his hair further and the clean scent drifts towards me. At least the scent of his blood is as vague as usual. Currently. "Did you leave your room after I walked away last night?" I ask.

"Why? Did you see me?" He straightens, attitude dropping. "I wasn't following."

"What?" I frown. "No, I didn't. Where were you?"

Rowan rests against the tree, sliding down slightly, and digging his unpolished shoes into the dirt. "I saw you and Grayson. You were together and went into the academy towards Sheridan House."

"You followed me? That was either brave or stupid, considering my mood when we parted."

"I waited outside the building, hoping you'd talk to me once you calmed down. Then changed my mind since I'm neither *brave nor stupid*." He gives me a pointed look. "Did you go into Grayson's room so he couldn't run when you confronted him? Or is there more between you and that's another reason you don't want the bond?"

Bond.

"My time with Grayson has nothing to do with your jealous theories."

He looks up and scoffs. "I'm not jealous. Not surprised either, but if Grayson wants to take on the ice queen challenge, good luck to him. I'm just concerned he's caught you in his lies."

Ice queen challenge? But he's telling the truth— annoyance, not upset, broadcasts across the space. "Let me be the judge of Grayson's ability to tell the truth, Rowan."

"Fine," he mutters. "Your funeral."

"Don't be ridiculous. Grayson won't kill me, and if he did, I expect I'm immortal," I reply. "I won't need a funeral."

He mutters to himself again and then gestures at me. "Have you returned Wes's toe? Again, I can't believe I'm saying those words."

"No. I haven't found time yet."

Rowan closes his eyes in a despairing way I'm learning to recognize. "See. Grayson distracted you from *that* last night. You'd better return the thing soon. I suppose you want to use me for help with sneaking back into the station?"

"Oh, I imagine I'll be in the police station very soon. In fact, I'm waiting right now."

"Why? What's happened?" He pulls himself from the tree. "Did someone find the toe?"

How do I put this?

"Why, Violet, this isn't a pause for dramatic effect, is it?" he asks snidely, echoing our time by the greenhouse.

"There's been another murder, Rowan."

Alarm hits his face. "What? Who? Bloody hell, Violet. You could've started our chat with that information." He steps closer. I back up. "Another student?"

"Rory. Killed the same way as Wesley," I say flatly. "Including the runic decoration."

"Crap." He swipes a hand across his hair. "How do you know this? I never heard anything at breakfast. If Thornwood or the police knew, they'd lock you up while waiting for Dorian!"

"I imagine I'll enjoy that pleasure later. Perhaps I could leave the toe behind at the station?"

"Droll. But how do you know?" he presses. "Did you see Rory's body when you ran into the woods?"

He *was* watching my every move.

"No. Grayson saw Rory's body last night. He was in the woods and—"

I startle as Rowan chokes out a strange noise and looks at me with yet more despair. "Violet! Are you insane? Grayson killed again."

"He did not," I retort.

"Why are you defending the guy?" He drags both hands through his hair and stands with elbows at right angles. "What does he have over you? I thought you'd be more resistant to mental magic."

"Grayson didn't kill! He isn't using magic on me," I say, shocked at my voice rising. "There wasn't any shifter blood on Grayson. Only his own."

"You can hardly scent blood, Violet." He drops his hands, eyes growing wider. "The vampire had blood on him and tricked you into thinking it was his, not a shifter's."

"No! I know the blood was Grayson's because I've tasted his," I blurt.

Rowan falls silent and holds a palm over his mouth, staring for a moment. His cheeks grow pink. "What?" he asks eventually. "*What?*"

"I bit Grayson and when I tasted—"

"Stop!" Rowan holds a hand up. "You hate being touched,

yet you're involved in blood play? With him? The guy must have a death wish if he's prepared to let you unleash on him."

Better than with you because that could become a real threat. "No. I bit his hand. Once. My tasting Grayson's blood isn't relevant."

"Um. Yes. It is. Very. No wonder you refused to listen to the truth about the guy." He rubs his temples. "Is that why you freaked out about the bond?"

"I don't want to talk about that topic," I say quietly. "Not yet."

"Well, I do," he replies loudly. "Don't be all 'Violet Blackwood' about this and behave like the situation only affects you and nothing else matters. The bond bloody well affects me too."

"Oh? Did the dam break that holds back all your emotional responses to people and now risks your dark part 'unleashing'?" He blinks. "No? I told you last night, your magic and the witch bond tore through everything that controls my nature. That's one reason I want to stay away from you, Rowan."

"This isn't all about what *you* want," he repeats. "There're two people involved."

"You clearly stated you'd never choose a bond with me, Rowan. I believe you called me 'the girl who doesn't give a shit about anybody but herself and doesn't care about me.'"

"Interesting that you remembered my precise words, Violet. Almost as if they upset you."

I stare. "Upset me? What upsets me is fate shoving this nightmare on us both. If the bond is affecting you as badly as it is me, we stay apart. Simple."

"Simple? Yeah, well, I don't think that's our choice, Violet," he retorts.

"I know. I can't keep away from you."

A still drops in the gathering storm. "You're accepting the bond?"

"No. I can't, because you're my alibi."

"Oh, nice." His face sours. "Whatever so-called dam I've broken hasn't washed away your rude, self-centered nature."

I take slow breaths, copying how Dorian deals with threats to his self-control. The bond naturally intensifies my reactions to Rowan. *Oh, how wonderful.* "Correct. At least part of myself is operating normally."

More grumbling beneath his breath. At least I'm not catching Rowan's thoughts—bonded witch instant mind-reading would be an unimaginable level of Hell.

"Well. I came here to inform you that human authorities will arrive to accuse me of murder again. Because Holly knows I was with you last night, not only are you an alibi, but a possible accomplice," I say, regaining control.

"What the fuck?" he breathes out.

"Like I said, Holly knows I planned to see you. If you're that upset with me, when the police interview you tell them you weren't with me all evening. Tell them I was with Grayson. Up to you. I don't care." Rowan makes a soft scoffing sound. "What?"

"Bonded witches, remember? I can't do anything that would threaten your safety." He steps towards me and looks down. "And I'm pissed that you think I would betray you if we *weren't* bonded."

I hold my breath against Rowan, against his magic, hoping, hoping, *hoping* I can't scent the guy's blood. I can't, but the hurt radiating towards me is confusingly strong and contradicts his current hostility. Leif told me there's more beneath Rowan's arrogance and now he's an open book to me.

And he's seeing between my pages too.

I clench my teeth. "Sorry?"

"Huh. Well. Thanks for being crystal clear about the situation. Glad I'm still useful."

"Rowan. I will still help with your spell before we stop

seeing each other. This was always an exchange of favors."
He makes a derisive noise. "Or don't you want my help?"

"A bargain is a bargain, Violet."

"And I will keep that bargain. Then we'll stay apart. I'm sure our distance will ensure this bond nightmare becomes easier with time."

His jaw drops as if I smacked him in the face. "Which will be easier for you than for me, Violet Blackwood."

"Why? How could you possibly want this constant conflict?"

Rowan moves closer still, his presence seizing me in a chokehold, blurring my mind until I can't find my magic. He looked at me like this the night in my room when I held him against the wall with a spell, but this time I'm the one immobile, not Rowan.

Yet there's no spell. Neither of us is trapped now. His steel-blue eyes stay fixed on mine, both of us refusing to move, caught in a different type of stalemate. Rowan's blood isn't calling to me, so why has my heart rate picked up?

"What would you do if I touched you?" he asks in a decidedly unromantic tone.

Our standoff continues for a few more seconds before I look away and break the connection, eager to leave. Silence follows me as I walk away.

I can't answer his question because I don't know any more.

Chapter Four

VIOLET

WHAT STRINGS DID DORIAN NEED TO PULL OR HOW MANY
necks did he threaten to wring to keep me out of human
police custody? Although, I do spend an inordinate amount
of time in a room at the station that I once visited and
plundered, interviewed by the two detectives who I insulted at
the barbecue.

The ones who witnessed Rory take hold of me and how I
fought back, got pissed and lost control.

Dorian couldn't be present, but he enlisted an attorney, a
witch who works at a law firm that's run by an old
acquaintance—whoever or whatever that means. The elderly
attorney soon gives up on telling me to keep my mouth shut,
so I hold back since leaving the station asap holds greater
importance. I'm distracted by other things—like a witch
bond, a desire for another vampire's blood, and missing
potions that could end in me attacking the detectives. That's
quite enough for one day without a murder charge too.

The Blackwood rune sets this murder firmly in the 'supes

did it' category, but after watching Kai and the shifters interact, he's crept onto my suspect list. He should be on my detective buddies' list too.

Dorian finally arrives, but not before the detectives tire of the interview and begrudgingly release me. I return to the academy under a barrage of questions from Dorian and Eloise. My father appears satisfied by my half-responses, but Eloise's silence means she isn't. The headteachers allow us a room to sit and talk in and Ms. Lorcan makes a sly comment about my lack of academic effort.

Seriously? As if that matters.

Vanessa's room.

I pull a face—I expect I'll see her soon too. Eloise sits on the sofa, and I take the chair Vanessa sat in yesterday. I've asked Eloise to speak to me alone first because I don't want another 'talking to' about recent events from both stern parents. Eloise whispered to me earlier that she has what I need, and I'm on edge waiting for her to give me the potion.

She produces the pink liquid in a clear medicine bottle and sets it on the table beside the half-empty tissue box. Immediately, I grab hold and take a swig.

Eloise's shaped eyebrows raise. "Violet. You're unlikely to attack someone from missing one dose."

I swallow, refasten the lid and slip the bottle into my pocket. "How do you know? What's the longest time between doses?"

"A day."

"That isn't long, Mother."

"You have some now. Panic over. Look after that potion, though. I don't have all the herbs I need for another batch— I'll find some, but that'll take a few days." I nod and sit on my hands. "Why did you want to talk to me alone, Violet?"

Voices from outside the room's open door filter into the silence and rather than meet Eloise's eyes I examine the sunflowers adorning the tissue box on the table.

The next words choke me. "I have a problem. I need help. That's why I don't want Dorian here." In my texts earlier, I begged her not to tell Ethan and Zeke either; I couldn't cope with a big family intervention.

Her eyes go wide. "You already attacked someone, Violet? Who?"

"No!" I chew my lip hard and look at the abstract picture on the wall above her head. "Your potion doesn't work against vampires."

"Well, of course it doesn't," replies Eloise. "There's no need because you won't attack one. Vampires only want each other's blood for intimate reasons."

I jerk as if someone jammed a steel rod up my spine. "Pardon?"

Eloise smiles and shifts forward in her seat. "Violet. Are you attracted to a particular vampire's blood and want relationship advice?"

"Good grief. No." *No.* I grit my teeth.

That small smile. She doesn't believe me. "Then how did you discover the potion doesn't work?"

"I bit a vampire. On the hand."

"Because you wanted his blood?"

"Because he annoyed me."

Eloise pinches the bridge of her nose. "Did we not deal with this behavior years ago, Violet? You don't bite people. Not without permission."

"He had hold of me and I didn't want him to," I protest.

"Excuse me, he did what?" growls Dorian. I startle and turn around to where he stands in the doorway behind me, the deadly creature as deceptively attractive as Eloise—apart from his blackening eyes. "Who touched you when you didn't want them to?"

I fight rolling my own eyes. Between the three of them, my fathers are impossibly protective. Thank the stars Eloise agreed not to involve the other two. "Nobody."

He bares his teeth. "That isn't what I heard you say to your mother."

"Another student," I mumble. "A vampire—I can protect myself."

"And how do you know this vampire isn't connected to the murders?" Dorian walks around and stands beside Eloise, arms crossed tight against his chest. "Someone trying to provoke you?"

What do I say? How much do I say? "No. He's an acquaintance."

Eloise arches a brow at me. "Is he?"

"Mother!"

Dorian drops his arms. "Are you..." He shakes his head. "What the hell do I call it, Eloise?"

"I'm eighteen years old. Call 'it' what you want. No, I am not partaking in any sexual activity with another student— vampire, witch, or human, of any gender. Nor am I 'dating' as these students like to say." I huff. "How could you think that?"

"You said the reason yourself," says Eloise. "You're eighteen."

"I am not like you two," I retort. "I'm not obsessed by sex."

"Good," says Dorian firmly. "You don't need that distraction when dealing with... this." Eloise sighs at him. "Who is this 'acquaintance' you bit?"

"I'd rather not say. And I was talking to Eloise privately, if you don't mind, Dorian."

"Violet," warns Eloise.

At this point, I'd rather provoke my father than have him push the issue. Telling him I have a Petrescu acquaintance? A relative of the vampire who subjected my family to brutality at Ravenhold and beyond? Dorian would be furious that I bit Grayson's hand rather than take the opportunity to tear out his throat.

"You don't usually request mother-daughter chats," says Dorian suspiciously.

"Perhaps you sending me to this academy has awakened something in me," I retort. "Oh, and put me in a situation where I'm prime suspect for two murders."

Dorian's face hardens. "You will not be blamed for this."

I've considered other's words—this whole situation could be connected to my father, or his council. Whatever else, the aftermath of these killings causes a rift between academy and town, between supes and humans, and both against shifters. Has Dorian inadvertently created this situation by placing me here?

"If Violet wants to talk to her mother alone, let her." Poor Eloise looks overjoyed that I'm finally warming to non-essential interaction with her. But this is essential, and my sudden desire for a Petrescu's blood is only half the issue.

There's the tiny issue called Rowan.

"I was leaving anyway," retorts Dorian. "I need to reiterate to the headteachers how they are to deal with this situation."

I pity them, considering Dorian walked out the door irritated.

Eloise smiles back at me. I'm closer to my mother than I suspect many teen girls are, but in a distant way. She's had patience and guided me; stepped in if my fathers became too overbearing. Eloise's magic tuition also distracted me from my vampire side but, unfortunately, not the necromancy obsession.

I trust her.

"Do you and Dorian have a witch bond?" I ask.

"Well, our bond is more because we share the same blood, Violet."

"But you knew each other when you were still only a witch, not a hybrid. Any bond then?" I press.

"Considering Dorian and I hated each other, we didn't

25

discover." Eloise purses her lips and I prickle under her scrutiny. "Are you asking if a hybrid could have a bond with another witch?" I already know the answer to that question. She leans across, one elbow on a knee, hand beneath her chin. "Is there a witch at Thornwood who you're bonded to?"

"Maybe," I mutter. "A witch and I shared magic energy to work on a spell and now I can't hurt him. He says we're bonded."

"Hurt him? Whatever for?" She frowns. "You can't be bonded if you want to harm the guy."

"Really?" I perk up. But do I? Once the fury and confusion wore off, I didn't want to harm Rowan. Maybe the test will come if somebody else hurts him.

"You touched a guy?" Eloise asks with quiet awe.

"I had to." I explain the situation to Eloise at a basic level, not mentioning Grayson's name or meeting him afterwards. She listens carefully, not speaking.

"Wanting a vampire's blood *and* physical contact with a witch? Quite a step forward, Violet. If somebody had told me either would happen a couple of weeks ago, I'd never believe them," she muses. "Perhaps we did make the right decision in sending you here."

"I don't want a romantic relationship with either guy, if that's what you mean," I say firmly.

"You'll discover that's difficult to resist for the two reasons you're drawn to the pair—blood and bond." She chuckles. "Violet Blackwood, collecting her consorts already."

I can't help the snarl that escapes my mouth. "Blood, bond, or whatever, I'm not connecting any further. Once the killer is caught, I'm leaving Thornwood. With or without your permission. Without *them*."

Eloise watches me quietly. If she's trying to read my expression to see hidden longing for either guy, she'll fail.

"If you *are* witch bonded to this guy, there's little you can do, Violet. Few bonded witches don't develop a physical relationship."

A shudder runs through me. "If I keep away from the witch, I can avoid the temptation should I have a sudden sexual awakening and desire more." I catch her amused look. "No. That is not happening."

She chuckles. "Who is this witch?"

"My alibi," I reply.

"Rowan Willowbrook?" She smiles. "One of the founding family lines Dorian doesn't dislike, fortunately for the witch. Who's the lucky vampire?"

"There is no 'lucky vampire'. My contact with his blood merely indicates that the potion doesn't work against vampires." She smiles rather than repeating her earlier comment. "I do not want anything from Grayson."

A quiet comes over Eloise, her smiles and delight that I'm moving forward in life snatched away. "Grayson Petrescu?"

Ah. Oh, dear. "Yes. I suggest you stop encouraging me to involve myself in a romantic entanglement with him. Or 'collect' him."

She blinks. "Grayson isn't closely related to Oskar, but the Petrescu name triggers Dorian every time it's spoken. The bad blood between the Petrescus and Dorian continues."

"Exactly. I'd rather not threaten Grayson's physical safety." I stand, unwilling to continue this further now that I've accidentally dropped a bombshell filled with a legacy of hatred. "Don't you dare tell Dorian about him."

"Why would that worry you if you don't care about Grayson?" Eloise's brow pinches. "He could be linked to events, Violet. You must tell us if there's any inkling this Petrescu is targeting you."

I'm torn between the Violet who holds back and suspects everybody to the one whose lust for Grayson's blood switches off my sensibilities. The first Violet remains in control—just —if I keep away from the guy.

"If Grayson Petrescu holds nefarious intentions towards me, Mother, I will deal with him."

But how? Succumb to the need that rises when I'm near him and lead him towards his death? No vampire could stop me killing, frenzied or not. The thought I'd harm Grayson disturbs me when this should satisfy me with an answer to the problem. Why?

Because the bond hasn't only broken the barrier that held back my Dorian side. I'm as much Eloise—the equally deadly hybrid, but one who cares about people and connects to her emotions. Having that unleashed in me is as abhorrent as suddenly becoming an uncontrolled killer.

I do not like this new Violet.

Chapter Five

VIOLET

By the end of that day, news rippled around the academy before building into a tidal wave of rumor that naturally hit me. Oddly, nobody mentions the rune, which means that information remains secret. Why? Dorian's insistence?

Kai and his friends are questioned the next day, since Dorian insists that authorities consider others as potential killers, but the police arrest nobody.

Dorian's influence stretches far and wide, but he can't influence everybody in our world. Some of those Dorian can't sway target him, always have and always will. Now that target is stuck to my back, which is totally unfair because even without the rune on Rory, every single finger continues to point my way.

At least Eloise replenished my potion and I can stay amongst others without tearing them apart. The bottle is now back in my trunk and re-secured with magic. I'd lost myself to complacency, as nobody else knew about the treatment I'd decided hiding the potion amongst Holly's paraphernalia would be safe.

How naïve of me.

This time, whoever touches the bottle will trigger magic that stains their fingers with a hidden ultraviolet glow. In fact, if anybody touches the trunk they'll likely burn.

I haven't heard from any of the guys since the news hit campus, although I do know that authorities took Rowan for questioning, asking him to corroborate my story. I'm fully prepared for Rowan to tell the truth—that I wasn't with him all night—but also know he won't. Witch bond.

Our conversation that day left me unsettled for reasons I both can and can't fathom. Rowan knows I've no desire to replace him with Grayson, so that helpfully avoids some conflict.

I shake my head. Replace him?

Despite keeping a physical distance from Rowan, he sends texts incessantly with veiled questions about my plans and reminders that even though I want nothing to do with him, I have to keep my end of the bargain and help him with his mysterious spell.

That's fair but the thought of our magic and hands touching again sends uncomfortable responses roaring through my body—fear that we'll solidify the bond further, and horror that Eloise is right and I won't be able to avoid a physical desire for him.

I don't intend to spend my whole life in celibacy, or without an understanding consort or two, but a life isolated hasn't offered opportunities, nor was I seeking any. I'd no interest in the human guys at the high school and they certainly had no interest in me. Disliking people touching me doesn't encourage intimacy—will that also change now that the bond has opened me up to the possibility I'll want Rowan?

And then what? My motherly chat hasn't helped at all. In

fact, she merely added more confusion. If _only_ the bond creates desire for Rowan rather than a personal affection, how can a romantic attachment not end badly? We already clash and I'd likely hurt Rowan since he isn't resisting our bond.

Yes, I'm insensitive to people, but I can now sense how Rowan feels, and I won't treat him any more unfairly than fate has treated us. Rowan can thank my Eloise side for that. Therefore, we need to maintain a distance and ensure I quash any chance we become emotionally closer.

I'll help Rowan with his spell, as promised, and perhaps we can decipher this code. Then I'll return to what I do best —remain detached. Once these murders are solved, I'll be out of all the guys' lives. Ties can easily be broken, even if bonds can't be.

I haven't seen Leif either. He left campus the day after, which at first aroused suspicion until his mother visited the academy to explain why. That information 'why', and where he is, isn't shared, and I'm irritated I only collected Rowan's and Holly's phone numbers. Last time we spoke, I upset Leif. What did he speak to Vanessa about—maybe she upset him too?

Considering that Rowan claims not to know where Leif is, he's awfully sure that the guy will return soon.

I'm curious but I've more important matters to deal with: my unwanted souvenir—one that I've brought to Wesley's funeral today. I snuck from the academy long before the funeral begins at 2PM, and now sit at the edge of the graveyard where I met Grayson that evening, far away from the path and partially secluded by a mausoleum. I've watched mourners arrive, itching to take photos or make notes, but so far resisting.

Grayson.

I'm confused whether I'm avoiding him due to the blood issue, or that he's avoiding me because he knows I'll nag him to tell his story. I'm building up to taking the risk I'll hurt him if I approach and listen to his tale. For now, I know whose blood covered Grayson and that needs to be enough.

Once I tick the funeral off my 'to do' list, he's next.

Less than a dozen guests file through the arched doorway into the small, gray-bricked church, all welcomed by the gray-haired and grave-faced vicar. I've no ability to empathize how losing a loved one would feel, partially because the chances this could happen are extremely low. Suffering the distress I'm witnessing can't be pleasant for these individuals, and no doubt the new 'open' Violet would feel this if someone in my life died.

I'm less than impressed when Rowan climbs over the wall at the edge of the graveyard, just as I'm about to sneak to the church and watch from the doorway. Why's he here? I never indicated to Rowan my intention to join the funeral party. He's dressed in his uniform, as I am, hoping the conformity will help should I be spotted. Yes, I'm distinctive if you interact with me, but from the back I could be one of a number of dark-haired students.

I'd hoped keeping away from Rowan for a few days might weaken the connection we made that night, but hairs stand up on my arms as he approaches, as I sense his magic reaching towards mine.

So, a worse reaction, not better. Great.

"What are you doing here?" I ask coolly.

"I knew *you'd* be here. I've come to take you back to the academy." He's stony faced, not looking at anything around us, as he stands over me.

"No." I hold his look, skin prickling at his attempt to call the shots again.

"You can't attend Wes's funeral service, Violet," he says, equally harshly.

"Why? Do you think the crucifixes might melt me?"

His lips remain thin. "I waste too much time on keeping you out of trouble. When will your stupidity end?"

"Excuse me?" I growl.

"You don't want to believe Grayson killed, so you're putting yourself at risk by constantly 'investigating' in places you shouldn't be seen."

"I'm not having another Grayson conversation," I say tersely. "And I'm not walking into the church to sit and enjoy the sermon. I'm staying out of sight to watch if anybody suspicious attends."

"Apart from *you*?" My face sours. "You don't know everybody, Violet."

"Yes, but I can spot anybody who isn't connected to the family. There're at least three people I've seen who've kept themselves separate and not approached Mr. Willis or his wife."

"Who?" Rowan peers at the church.

"Have I piqued your interest?"

"No. They're probably detectives or representatives from the supernatural council. *We* shouldn't be here. What if detectives are around for the same reason—looking for suspicious people? Again, such as you."

"Oh. I already saw them." He stares at me. "That's why I stayed out of the church until everybody walked inside."

"Right. We're leaving. Now." Rowan curls fingers around my upper arm and I jerk at the contact. Not only because he put his hands on me, but because the same powerful magic as the night we last touched jolts me.

His fingers press harder, expression sharing my surprise for a few moments before I pull my arm away.

Rowan rubs his hand as if I burned him and his touch still tingles beneath my skin, even through my blazer. "Shit," he gasps.

"What's wrong?"

"Are you seriously asking me that question?" he mutters. "Violet. Please. Leave."

"I'm staying."

33

The pallbearers with Wesley's dark wood coffin now move slowly from the church, and I refocus my attention, shuffling further out of the sight of mourners. I recognize one of the tall guys at the front as a bully Grayson attacked that night. The other pallbearers bear similarities to the Wallis family, dark hair sprouting from the stockily built men's sleeves.

"Wait!" I grab Rowan's blazer. "Look."

The mourners, led by Wesley's parents, follow the pallbearers around the side of the church, towards the freshly dug plot at the edge of my view. Mr. Wallis's arm wraps around his wife's shoulders, helping her stay upright and two other couples stand around the plot, hands linked together, and heads bowed.

All wear black and solemn expressions, although Mrs. Wallis hides hers beneath a wide-brimmed hat with a short tulle veil. Witches never wear black at funerals—Eloise forced me to put on a pretty red dress for the only one I attended.

One where my parents kept me well away from the casket.

As the white-robed vicar begins his sermon, crunching footsteps turn my attention towards the gates to the graveyard. Viggo strides purposefully along the pebbled path, a lackey either side, the three scruffy shifters in their jeans and T-shirts out of place amongst the well-dressed mourners.

Out of place altogether.

Chapter Six

VIOLET

"What the hell?" whispers Rowan.

Without a second thought, I dart from my hiding place and take a new one beneath the church eaves, closer to the scene. Rowan's by my side in moments and I throw him a warning look—*don't try to make me leave.*

I peer around the corner of the church wall. Viggo and friends haven't approached the mourners but instead loiter nearby, pretending to look at gravestones. Those invited to the funeral are focused on the next part of their human burial ritual, and I bite away an inappropriate smile. Something's brewing that might help me.

"Now we definitely need to go," says Rowan.

"No," I reply. Rowan doesn't respond and I turn to see him resting his back against the church wall, looking up at the cloudy sky and taking deep breaths. "You can go. After all, you didn't want to be here."

"I'm not leaving you," he says through gritted teeth.

"Then keep quiet." He twists his head to me and I catch

another shocked expression before I crane my neck towards unfolding events.

Nothing happens immediately, and I pull out my phone to type notes. So much more useful than a pen and paper.

"I can't believe Viggo's here," whispers Rowan.

"I'm sure he isn't at the funeral to pay his respects." Viggo's louder voice interrupts me, Rowan, and everything, as it echoes through the quiet graveyard. "And here we go."

I edge around the wall, no longer worried I'll be spotted because all focus shifts to the unwanted arrivals.

"I'm guessing Rory won't get a memorial service or a funeral attended by important people?" Viggo keeps his distance—just—flanked by the two hulking shifters. "Nobody mentioned one. Shifters are second-class citizens *again*."

"Crap," says Rowan, close to my ear.

Wesley's mother clutches harder to his father, his face now a mask of horror. The burial plot blocks the town mayor's path to the shifters, and he makes to move around the edge, but a woman in another over-large hat stops him.

The two detectives I spotted earlier stand at a respectful distance to the funeral party, close to the back of the graveyard, but watch every movement. The gray-haired one looks over and I give him a small wave. He doesn't return my friendly greeting.

"This isn't an appropriate time to air your grievances, Viggo." A softly spoken man in a tailored black suit treads away from the shocked mourners towards the shifters.

"Like you ever listen to us at your council," Viggo sneers.

"Again, this is not the time or place." The well-groomed man is middle-aged, shorter than the unwanted guests but muscular, and I catch a flash of an expensive gold watch as he straightens his tailored suit sleeves. "Naturally, Rory's death is as great a concern to us all as Wesley's."

"Yeah, I doubt that. Shifters hospitalize local humans," whispers Rowan.

Viggo scoffs. "Rory was a shifter. You don't give a crap about us." The man approaches the angry guy and puts a hand on his shoulder to escort him further from the mourners. "Get your fucking hands off me, Sawyer."

"I understand you're upset, but please leave." The soft tone now holds an edge of menace, and Sawyer doesn't remove his hand. "Come to my offices tomorrow and we can discuss a suitable memorial for Rory. If your elders are amenable."

"I'm not visiting that factory! Your family built that on our land!" Viggo's voice rises again. At least the two guys with him have the decency to look awkward. "I bet your fucking son was involved in Rory's death."

"I suggest you don't make false accusations." The man flicks out a business card. "Contact me tomorrow. Go."

Behind him, the vicar continues his sermon, encouraging everybody to ignore Viggo, but failing as everything focuses on Sawyer and the shifters.

"This guy really is unbearably unpleasant and stupid," I say.

"I reckon he's drunk," says Rowan.

"Who's the man he's talking to?"

"Christopher Sawyer. Kai's father. He has issues with the shifters—the younger ones often vandalize his factory, and Sawyer has to employ heavy security. Bad blood. You really haven't gotten far with your detective work, have you?"

I flash him a look. "I know Kai's father is on the council, but never met the man. How could I know what he looks like?"

"Right. Then you'll know the Sawyers are the wealthiest family in the town?" I press my lips together. "No? Isn't Kai on your suspect list?"

"I had no real reason to suspect human involvement in Wesley's death," I retort. "Kai moved up the list after Rory died, but I haven't investigated him yet."

"And now?"

"Further up. But I'd need to figure out his motive to kill Wesley too, since there's no obvious one." I eye where Kai's father and Viggo have a terse conversation, now further away and beneath a willow tree. Then I look to the detectives. How much do they know about town politics? Because I don't know enough.

"We should leave while everybody's distracted, Violet," urges Rowan and attempts to take my hand, then sighs when I shove both into my pockets. "The detectives know you're here."

"They know I'm investigating too."

"As you're the main suspect, lurking near the funeral isn't sensible," Rowan reminds me.

I rest against the church wall and watch the burial rites recommence. How long does this take? "I need to stay until everybody leaves."

"What? Why?"

"Because I need to visit Wesley's grave."

Not only do I notice how suddenly Rowan goes quiet, but I annoyingly sense his panic. "No, Violet," he says eventually. "You've macabre ideas and curiosities, but that's too far."

"Why? Do you think I intend to dig him up?" I meet his horrified eyes. "Good grief, Rowan."

"It's impossible to tell with you. What if you want to 'investigate' Wes's body further?"

Rowan's look of alarm becomes wan-faced horror when I produce a plastic bag from my pocket. "Wesley's toe."

"I can see that."

"I want to return this to Wesley. The grave is freshly dug. I can bury his toe beside him."

Rowan swipes a hand down his face, mouth falling open. "Every time I move closer to understanding you, Violet, you hit me with something more."

I tuck the toe back into my pocket. "There's no point trying to understand me, Rowan. Nobody does."

"Including yourself, Violet Blackwood."

Rowan's close again and I avoid his eyes, where the truth about who we are lives. My attention on the shifters' invasion distracted me for a few minutes, but awareness snaps back to us as our auras wind together.

I step away. "I'm staying in town. Go back to the academy if you like; you don't need to stay with me."

Rowan pushes his tongue against his top teeth. "You don't understand me either, Violet. I'm staying, but can we at least leave the graveyard before the detectives walk over and start asking questions?" I open my mouth to respond but he silences me with, "I'll take you to see Leif—if you join me for something to eat."

"Leif?" I ask, voice rising. "You know where he is and never told me?"

"I'm telling you now."

"Another Rowan bargaining chip?" I snap.

And there it is. The Rowan smirk. "I know a great cafe."

As I glower at him and his eyes fill with smug amusement, I'm even more pissed that I'm bonded to this guy. We're too much alike and he keeps outsmarting me.

Chapter Seven

GRAYSON

VIOLET AVOIDS ME, WHICH CONFIRMS THAT SHE HAS THE SAME response to my blood as I do to hers. The night Rory died, and she tasted my blood, Violet tried to hide herself as she always does, but I easily sensed that something else affected her. Has Rowan stepped out of line? Surely if he had, Violet would squash him beneath her boot.

In fact, Violet avoided everyone but Holly for the last few days, especially me, and rarely attended class. That isn't unusual but recently she'd involved herself a bit more in academy life. Rory's murder isn't as focal as Wes's, but the kids still talk as if Violet killed them both. Dorian and Eloise visited the academy shortly after the murder's reveal—have they instructed their daughter to distance herself?

I caught a glimpse of Dorian this time, but only from behind. He walked as if he had no time for anybody, Eloise by his side and Violet the other—the three hybrids who all look a similar age rather than parents and child. Whenever Violet speaks about them, she rarely calls them 'Mom' or

'Dad'. But seeing her with Dorian reminds me exactly who Violet is and whose powers she inherited.

People should be frightened of Violet, not scornful or patronizing. Hell, Violet could terrorize the school if she wanted, but her obsession with controlling herself becomes more obvious to me. Still, I've seen Violet's vampire desire for blood—my blood. Did she realize her eyes darkened when she looked at me? That her own flowed closer to the surface?

Since I first caught Violet's scent, I've obsessed over tasting her blood and admit I avoided her as much as she did me after our encounter in my room. Violet's complete disinterest confused me and I stayed away, partly annoyed, until I decided that her disinterest is a good thing.

But now? I've held the girl, covered myself in her scent and triggered an aching unlike anything before. If I'd had one sure sign that Violet wanted to take a step forward after she tasted my blood, she wouldn't have left my room in a hurry that night.

But her barriers are back up and disdain firmly in place. Or is she *that* skilled in hiding how she feels she manages to hide something this major?

Only barely—that's why she keeps away from me.

I saw her sneak from campus today, and as Wes's funeral took place this afternoon, I only needed one guess where. Although tempted to follow her, I held back, especially when I saw Rowan head away from the academy less than an hour later. The pair haven't returned by early evening, and I question why I'm on alert for Violet when she doesn't want to see me.

Violet asked to hear my story the night Rory died, but something about me bothered her so much that she dropped her investigative line of inquiry and ran. Did scenting the blood as mine not Rory's give her enough reason to 'eliminate' me as a suspect? No. That isn't the reason she behaved out of character and ran before she found answers. My effect on her caused that.

In a way, Violet's decision not to return to me and ask more is hurtful. But what else can I expect from Violet Blackwood? I've built her in my mind as someone who'd grow closer to me with our new connection and realized how ridiculous that is.

I've watched her avoid Rowan too, so he's a determined guy following her today. They've similarities on a basic level—weird, reclusive, take no crap from anybody. Is there something more? Rowan's known for messing with people and for his dangerous magic. Few saw him help Violet at the memorial, but I did. I watch the pair closely, especially Rowan.

I could look for them tonight but I've an unavoidable meeting. Violet's comment comes to mind 'a meeting between you and somebody's jugular?' Is she unintentionally amusing? Sometimes it's hard to tell between deadpan seriousness and sarcasm.

A badly handled meeting with someone's jugular months ago got me into the mess I'm in now.

I'm not commanded to attend these sessions, but missing them wouldn't be sensible, and my uncle and his friends will find me anyway. I also don't want another 'Petrescu' slip up—my family is obsessed by the black mark I smeared on their name. My presence at Thornwood is supposed to help wipe away their bad history, which worked well at first until I edged towards hemia maturity. I don't need blood—not yet. That becomes my only diet once the desire for food dies away. Two years, tops.

I'm hemia but 'blood born' not made, something only the purest of vampires can achieve; those who date back to the originals. It's prestigious to carry and birth a vamp child and more common than humans realize. Lamia and pneuma vamps easily do the same but as always, humans fear the blood drinkers over those that feed on sexual and mental energy.

So, here I am. The new blood born Petrescu carrying the weight of my family's misdeeds, but also their hemia poor control.

I didn't mention Violet when she first arrived, but Josef and his buddies were well aware of her presence around town and the academy, even before the night of Wesley's murder. My uncle only mentioned her in passing, but they were in the area that evening and would be capable of the crime.

Revenge against the Blackwood by taking down his daughter?

Possible.

The place I meet them couldn't be more opposite to the exclusive London apartment or family estate in the countryside that he usually lives in. But if you're luring victims, you need them away from town and other people.

Or should I say, potential victims.

My uncle parked his distinctive red sports car behind the farmhouse, beside the large building once used as stables. That and the lights shining inside the single-story brick building tell me he's here.

I take a steeling breath and walk to the door at the front of the house. Unlocked. The three will be inside, but will they have a human with them tonight?

The door opens into a narrow hallway that leads towards a kitchen and lounge area, the blue carpet worn and faded, cream-colored paint peeling from the walls. The kitchen isn't in any better condition, an old-fashioned stove and square sink with a permanently dripping tap set in a chipped counter, a small fridge beside it.

I know the kitchen well from the time these people locked me in here but haven't used the room any of the times I've returned. Every visit, I bring with me the fear that they might lock and ward me inside the building again, but each time I return free of human and witch blood scent, I'm allowed to leave after our meeting.

In the other room, Josef Petrescu stands by the empty fireplace, hands in pockets, and turns his head when he senses me approach. The same two friends are with my uncle tonight—I've only heard their names a couple of times, and they rarely speak. Simeon and Ben. I think. They're vamps too—hemia, part of our extensive family line judging by their dark hair and pale skin—and the eyes, of course.

Looks like Josef doesn't intend to touch me himself tonight since he wears a dark suit, but the others are in jeans and plaid shirts unbuttoned over black T-shirts. Did Josef come straight from the city after a day's work?

Josef inclines his head. "Good evening, Grayson. I do hope you're not planning to run again tonight." He's softly spoken, a hint of the Slavic accent that I once thought set him as one of the old, original vampires. I later discovered he never left the family estate and so adopted a stronger accent.

"Run? That depends how hard you hit me," I reply, remaining in the doorway.

Where's the human? Josef always brings a human. He chuckles at my confusion as he catches my thoughts. "Less temptation for you tonight."

"Isn't that the point of these meetings?" I slide my hands in my jeans pockets.

"Do sit." He gestures at a tattered armchair.

Suspicious that tonight they'll trap me, I do as he says. "I haven't touched a witch or human."

Ben laughs gruffly.

"We did hear about the local deaths." Josef leans against the fireplace's mantle. "I'm surprised *you're* not accused considering your history."

"I was interviewed."

He nods. "Then the Blackwood girl is already killing? Seems she shares her father's traits."

"There's no proof."

"Mmm." Josef looks to Simeon who shifts in his seat, and I tense, ready to duck if he grabs me. "She'll slip up."

Why aren't they dragging me into the basement? The human must be down there, enthralled and bleeding.

"What's happening? Why am I here?" I ask.

"We're happy with your progress, Grayson." Josef smiles. "It would seem the right amount of pain discourages you."

"And locking me up and starving me?"

My sabbatical from Thornwood? Trapped in this house, only visited by them twice a week, each time offered a human to fend off my starvation. I was and still am confused—the imprisonment brought forward my desire for blood over food, yet they're punishing me for what they provoked.

After the witch girl almost died, and I therefore reinforced our family's reputation as violent in nature, my father removed the uncontrolled Petrescu kid from the academy. Then my uncle offered to help.

At first, I thought my treatment was punishment, but it didn't take long to figure out I'm undergoing twisted aversion therapy. Every time my vampire urges reacted to the bleeding human they presented to me; his delightful friends would hurt me. They fucking tortured me to the point that one of them only had to produce a knife for my body and mind to freeze.

The fear they've instilled keeps me away from all witches and humans as much as I can, terrified something might trigger the bloodlust. There's no vampire with a knife happy to slice into my flesh at the academy, but each time I return to him, Josef would know if I'd taken blood. They'd scent the witch or human.

Fuck, the bastards even killed me once, and I learned that despite immortality, death is painful and frightening. I believed my uncle when he looked into my dying eyes and said he'd burn me and permanently end my immortal life. All this for smearing a name the Petrescus' try to polish.

Now, each time I'm summoned, I don't know if death waits—temporary or permanent.

When I'm not at this house, everything feels like a distant nightmare, packed away in a box in my mind.

"If there's no 'treatment' tonight, why am I here?" I repeat.

"Last time we met, you mentioned Violet Blackwood had approached you."

I can't figure out his tone and have no chance of reading his mind. Has Josef read *mine*? Because if he has, he'd know I approached Violet first.

"We share classes."

"And outside of class?" He scratches his cheek with a long fingernail. "Are you friendly?"

"I'm not interested in Violet, if that's what you're implying."

The pause. I hate when they're quiet as much as when they shout, unable to hear their silent communications between each other. If Josef's about to tell me to keep away from Violet, life will become more unbearable.

"Does she like you?" asks Josef.

I can't help laughing at his question, but immediately shut my mouth when he throws me a poisonous look. "Violet doesn't like anybody."

"But she needs to like you."

An icy finger runs down my spine. "What do you mean?"

"Get close to her. Befriend Dorian Blackwood's precious offspring." His face hardens along with his tone. "If you succeed, we can pause your treatment for a while."

The ice spreads. "I can't make her spend time with me. Violet's magic surpasses any mind-control skills I have."

"Find another reason to get close," he snaps back. "Everybody has a weakness."

"Maybe she could have a weakness for you," says Simeon, and Ben shares his laughter.

"Believe me, Violet has no interest in a physical relationship of any kind." I moisten my lips. But she does—how long can she resist my blood?

"Well, find a way." Josef steps towards me. "Watch her. Tell me what Violet does and who with."

"I'm not screwing round with a Blackwood," I protest. "What do you think will happen to me if Violet or her father realizes a Petrescu is spying on her?"

Because that's what they're asking me to do. Why?

"That's a risk I'd rather *you* took, not me," Josef says tersely.

We lapse into silence. There's no point arguing, but that doesn't mean I'll do what they ask. I tip my chin. "If you want to mess with Dorian's kid, does that mean you're also involved with the local murders?" I glance between the three of them.

More silence.

"Ludicrous accusation, Grayson. How would we get to Violet if she's imprisoned or taken back to her family home?" Josef crosses his arms.

Get to. "You'd cause trouble for the Blackwoods if you did this and implicated her." I stand. "I'm trying to lose the taint attached to our name, as I thought you were. I'm not helping you with whatever this is."

Familiar anger flickers across his face and, still looking at me, he holds a hand out to stop Ben and Simeon, who've started to rise from the sofa. "I'd threaten you with a short stay in the basement, but that won't aid my plans."

I'm only half-paying attention to Josef, focused on which direction the others' attack might come from. Planning how to get the fuck out.

"But do remember how unpleasant Ben and Simeon can be when you upset me, Grayson."

Remember? I'm as tortured by the images as I was by their hands when they leak into my mind. Even on days I manage to suppress the horrific memories, the slightest distraction can trigger them again.

"Does my father know about any of this? Does he want me to watch Violet too?" I've asked them over and over, unwilling to believe that Josef could hide these actions from him. But then my father never visits me at the academy, nor is he around most times I'm home between semesters. I once asked my father if he'd seen Josef recently and he denied he had. Genuinely—I couldn't detect a hint of anything hidden.

"You've been warned what will happen if he does discover our meetings." Josef inclines his head at Ben.

One day I'll torture and kill Josef in the exact way he abuses me—only I'll finish him with fire. Once I figure out whether he acts alone or someone more powerful pulls the strings, I'll walk up to Dorian's council and tell them. Then hope Dorian agrees to keep one Petrescu safe while he deals with my uncle.

For now, I deal with the two vampires lunging at me as Josef watches.

Violet.

She'll be the death of me, I swear.

Chapter Eight

VIOLET

I RARELY FREQUENT HUMAN CAFES, BUT I'VE VISITED THIS ONE with Holly a couple of times. The half-empty place Rowan takes me to is at the opposite end of town from the graveyard —modern, but themed as if a hundred years old, with old style mahogany dressers and shelves filled with books. Round tables and wooden chairs fill the maroon and black painted premises. I peruse the owners, expecting vamps, but no. Only humans are behind the small counter serving the pungently greasy food.

After ordering from the laminated menu, I'd positioned myself at the rear of the cafe, on an uncomfortable chair at a freshly wiped table and waited for my pasta. Now the plates and bowls lie empty in front of us, and I'm particularly impressed how Rowan can eat such a large burger and mound of fries.

But I'm more interested in watching those who come and go than the quality of the cuisine. Perhaps Viggo might visit?

"Will you become a blood drinker?" asks Rowan.

"That was blunt. How do you know I don't consume blood already?" I sip from the half-empty cup of sickly sweet soda.

"You don't. I presume you use magic to stop yourself, since a teen version of Dorian wouldn't be in control." He scrunches up a white paper napkin and drops it onto his ketchup-streaked plate.

"Not magic." I narrow my eyes. "Do you know about my tonic? Did you steal it?"

"What?"

"Well, you've tried to take my things before," I say accusingly. "And someone took the bottle."

Rowan's brow pinches. "Bottle of what, Violet?"

"I drink something daily that dulls the scent of blood and ensures I don't desire the taste." I set the glass down. "Somebody stole the potion."

Rowan sits bolt upright. "You haven't taken any recently? What will happen? Are we safe?"

"Calm down; I'm not on the verge of performing a town massacre. Eloise already replaced the potion." My lips thin. "Someone took the bottle from my room, which is locked in the daytime. Somebody in the academy with a key or magic, and who knows I use a potion."

"Interesting." Rowan taps his fingers on the table. "You need a better hiding place."

"Thank you for your obvious statement. I didn't think I'd need to hide the potion."

"I stand by my theory that somebody is screwing with you to screw with your father and his council." Rowan rests back in his seat. "They're setting you up. You were seen clashing with both Wes and Rory the days they died."

"Yes. I've reached that conclusion, but my father has enemies all over and amongst all races. That hardly narrows down our possible suspects." As Rowan nods and drinks, I watch him. "We could get some evidence from Rory's—"

"No!" Rowan startles me. "No way, Violet." He leans forward. "If more body parts disappear from corpses, the authorities will think the serial killer is collecting trophies."

"Firstly, Rowan, this isn't a serial killer until he or she murders three or more people. Secondly and anecdotally, a serial killer would take a trophy at the time of the murder."

He shakes his head. "Well. Let's hope the murders stop at two."

"I expect there'll be more." I pull out my phone and peruse notes from my earlier experiences at the funeral. "We need to predict who will die next or find the murderer first." Silence. I glance up. "Yes?"

I'm detecting a lot of shock from Rowan today. "I bloody hope you're wrong."

I shrug. "Until I'm properly framed, the killer needs to continue."

"You almost sound like you want more murders," he says hoarsely.

"Good grief. Do you think I like death to the extent I'm happy for people to die?"

"I don't understand you, remember?" he says pointedly.

"About Leif," I say, pushing the conversation back from the edge of 'us'. "I've eaten with you, while you pretended that I did so by choice. Now tell me where he is."

I bristle as Rowan's attention shifts to something on our left, and only when somebody approaches the table do I see why he didn't answer.

A recognizable guy with brown hair flopping across his face drags a chair from a nearby table and sits. Several guys and girls crowd around that table, all in the local high school uniform. One girl with brown hair in a ponytail squeaks and slaps a guy's hand as he helps himself to her fries.

I fight rolling my eyes—at the dumb human behavior and Kai's arrival beside us.

"Hey. Rowan, right?" asks Kai. "And Violet?"

"Yeah," Rowan replies cautiously. "We've met before."

"Really? Huh." He points between us. "Wanted to say, I loved your magic at the memorial. Those shifters need pulling into line."

"Well, it would appear that someone pulled Rory into line," I interrupt. "In a rather permanent fashion."

Rowan clears his throat and shakes his head at me.

Kai shrugs. "Probably killed by his own." For once, I'm silenced. "Rory might've stepped out of line, and you heard what Viggo said. I've seen the mess the assholes make of people who they decide deserve a kicking."

"Why? Rory seemed to be one of Viggo's closest... whatever they are," I reply.

Kai frowns. "You should be happy with the theory. This takes the heat off you."

Since the moment Kai sat down, I've bristled at his audacity and itch to shut him up and ensure he leaves us alone. I have a toe to bury and information to extract from Rowan so I can see Leif. But isn't this what I want—for Kai to talk? Therefore, I must act semi-normally for as long as I can endure.

"Anyway. Party at my house tomorrow. Extending an invitation." Kai grins at Rowan. "You're always welcome, now we know whose side you're on."

Rowan's eyes widen, his alarm hitting me. "You mean the memorial? I was protecting Violet."

Soda spurts across the table from my mouth as I choke at Rowan, who glares back.

Kai looks between us and laughs too. "Sure, you were."

Stay calm. Do not be weird. I slant my head and study my new suspect further. He oozes confidence; the guy's attractive —for a human—with the self-assured attitude of someone who's popular and very much aware he is. I bet Kai's wealth helps attract friends.

Mental note for later: if he's inviting Rowan, Kai isn't the one threatening people to keep away from supes. "Are many from the academy invited to your party?" I ask.

He flicks a look at me. "Why? Do you want to come?"

"I'd rather scoop my eye out with this spoon than endure the horrors of adolescent hedonism."

Blank look. Another mental note: Kai's intelligence level appears too low for a sophisticated killer.

"You trust your guy to go alone?" Kai smirks at Rowan. "Everybody comes to my parties for a good time. Guaranteed."

I blink. "My what? Do you mean him?"

"Could you sound anymore disgusted, Violet?" Rowan snaps. "Yeah, I'll come. For a *good time*."

Am I missing something? Aren't all parties for a good time? Unless you're an antisocial loner and then it's a decidedly bad time.

"Is Holly invited?" I ask.

"Yeah. Holly always gets an invite."

"Will Ollie be there?"

"No clue. I haven't seen Ollie for a couple of days."

"Oh. I hope he isn't dead." Kai gawks. "What? There does appear to be a homicidal maniac loose in town. One who doesn't discriminate when choosing a victim."

"Nah. I've seen him but haven't *seen* him." He laughs at my confusion. "In school. Ollie's avoiding me."

Curiouser and curiouser. Yet I am rather impressed with myself that I've managed to speak to this person for several minutes without repelling them.

"You know where my place is, Rowan. Everybody knows. Tomorrow at eight?" Kai nods at me. "If you change your mind, Violet, you're welcome."

"Unlikely. I'm rarely welcome anywhere." I drain my soda. "But I have a question for you."

"Yeah?"

"A shifter died. Your party may seem insensitive—almost like a celebration. Doesn't that worry you?"

Kai pulls a non-committal face. "Their problem, not mine. Our lives don't stop because other people are having a bad time."

A bad time? "And you feel safe considering recent violent events?"

"Why wouldn't I? Nobody dares touch me."

"I believe Wesley deceived himself with the same thought, Kai. What if you're next?"

Rowan kicks me under the table, and I stomp on his foot with my heavy shoes. "Fuck, Violet," he mumbles as he winces.

"If I were you, I'd shut up," says Kai icily.

"Is that a demand?" I retort.

"Yeah." He glowers.

"I don't follow demands, Kai. I rarely entertain suggestions. Certainly not those from the mouth of a human with inferior intellect who buys his popularity." Satisfied I've shut him up, I stand. "I'm bored now, Rowan. I have something more important than your social life." I edge past Kai, subtly pressing against his mind for any telling images.

The emptiness inside male human heads reveals itself again.

"Kai's right, you need to learn when to keep your mouth shut," says Rowan as he holds open the café door for me.

"I tried to be nice."

"Nice? You called him stupid."

"After I got the answers I wanted, I ceased the pleasantries. They were no longer necessary." He raises his eyes skyward. "Why did you kick me?"

"To get your attention."

I pause as the door closes behind him. "Like pulling pigtails?"

"No, Violet. Like, stop sounding weird."

"Even you must know you're asking the impossible, Rowan." I blow air into my cheeks. "I need to bury the toe now."

"Bloody hell," mutters Rowan as he follows me. "What am I doing?"

Rowan does seem to mutter a lot when we're together.

Behind, Kai leaves the café, as loud as Wesley the night he died. With each layer I peel back from this town, I discover another conflict. The party by the fire? Not as harmonious as it appeared.

I gaze up at the cloud-covered sky that interested Rowan. If people in this town can't see the gathering storm within their community, they won't be prepared for the destruction when it hits.

Chapter Nine

VIOLET

"I can *not* believe I'm here," says Rowan, and I look back to where he stands in the shadows by the church, dragging fingers through his messy hair. The night sky is delightfully dark, moonlight absent, leaving me to perform my task in shrouded peace.

Toe successfully placed in the burial site, I back away and return to Rowan whose stern expression confuses me. "You don't agree this is the right thing to do?"

He snorts. "The *right thing to do* would be not taking the toe in the first place. Let's leave. Quickly."

"I wonder what happened when somebody noticed Wesley's missing toe?" I tramp back towards the path. "Or do you think the mortuary staff replaced his socks so nobody could see?"

"You've thought way too much about this, Violet." Rowan strides ahead and I hurry to catch up.

"Now. Where's Leif?" I ask. "Are you taking me to him as bargained?"

"Leif's staying with a family friend on the other side of town for a few days. He'll be back at the academy soon."

"I thought he wanted to leave Thornwood altogether."

Rowan side glances me. "Anybody who mysteriously leaves Thornwood permanently right now would be tracked down and arrested."

Although Leif's absence remains suspicious to me, I've dropped my other suspicion that Rowan mind-controlled his friend. Now I've a greater connection to the witch, I'm more able to sense if he's lying. Fortunately, we don't have the ability to communicate telepathically like some bonded witches do; I'd go insane if I had someone in my head. Especially one who takes pleasure in annoying me.

"Why is Leif hiding?" I ask.

"Because the shifters are giving him grief again, and now that Rory's dead, they'll be worse than ever. You saw Viggo and heard how he spoke to Leif."

"Hmm. He's worried for his safety? Isn't Leif safest at Thornwood where there aren't any shifters?"

Rowan goes quiet until we reach the pathway outside the graveyard. "Everything's more complicated than Viggo. I've told Leif a few times that he should explain to you."

"But he hasn't."

"Leif doesn't speak to many people. His half-shifter status causes issues, and he doesn't like to talk about them. I've told him he can trust you and that maybe you can help."

"Me?" He asked in art class that time and I rejected him, naturally. "Leif knows not to bother asking."

Rowan chuckles and shakes his head. "Yeah, he laughed at me when I made the suggestion, but you like a good mystery. And yes, I'm taking you to Leif. I sent him a message earlier explaining we're in town and that we'd head over."

As we walk, Rowan wanders closer, and I'm annoyingly pulled back to the moment our witch souls recognized each other. I'm not responding as I would to Grayson, but there's an energy in Rowan's aura that tugs at mine. I've concluded that if we've a bond, Rowan and I are magical magnets attracted to each other. Nothing more. Still, I edge to one side.

As darkness falls, less cars drive through the streets, but I definitely remember more people moving along the sidewalks at this time in my past visits. Usually, kids from the academy would gather at the bus stop to return to the campus around this time, but nobody sits on the bench beneath the shelter.

"Kai might not bother, but people are worried," says Rowan.

I halt. "Can you read my mind?"

"No, Violet, but I sense you're confused. Humans tend to hide at night when there's a serial—" He pauses and smiles as I open my mouth to correct him. "A couple of unsolved murders."

"The race has *some* common sense then." I gesture ahead. "How far to this house Leif is staying in?"

"Other side of the woods, but we are not taking a shortcut through there." Rowan gives me a warning look. "Otherwise, I won't take you to Leif. Okay?"

My jaw clenches at his tone. "Okay."

Rowan hunches against the cooler breeze, blazer collar turned up. The weather has no effect on me, and neither will the distance. I'd rather not walk to this house and instead travel at my personal speed, but Rowan would never keep up.

A solitary car passes as we head along the sidewalk that runs out through the edge of the town.

"You should come to Kai's party," Rowan suggests.

"Don't be ridiculous."

"Not even for a little sleuthing?"

Of course, Rowan knows that I'd considered this, but I've weighed that up against mind-numbing social interaction and the time that would waste. "I'll send you to investigate and you can report back to me."

He chuckles. "That's presumptuous of you to believe I'd help."

"I'm sure Nancy Drew had helpers," I say pointedly. "And I'm not impressed by that so-called joke. I actually tried to find her."

Rowan's laugh fills the emptiness. "I will never grow bored of pushing your buttons, sweet Violet," he says, and I snap my head around to glare at him. "I've enjoyed our lovely afternoon and evening together, although on our next date, I suggest somewhere more pleasant than a graveyard."

Pushing my buttons. Date. I ignore him.

The park gates come into view and they're open with the shrouded woods beckoning. As we pass, Rowan says, "No," as if warning a child to stay put, and I hiss at him. Of course, he laughs.

The shifter scent hits me before I register their presence, one of them barreling from the dark and knocking Rowan to the ground. I'm barely able to respond before the powerful guy grabs the back of Rowan's blazer and drags him through the gates into the shadows he emerged from.

A deeply seated anger bursts into my veins as Rowan's body disappears into the night, and I race after the pair, summoning magic instinctively. The shifter sprawls forward onto the ground, releasing his hold on Rowan's clothes as my invisible bolt hits him in the back. A winded Rowan struggles to his feet.

"What are you doing?" I yell at the shifter and march over. Before the asshole can move, I slam a spell into his back again, fire also sparking across my fingertips. "Didn't you learn what a hybrid is at the memorial?"

Panting, the shifter pushes onto his hands and knees and looks over his shoulder at me, sneering. "We're not scared of you, little bitch."

"Watch your fucking mouth," shouts Rowan.

Fire flares in his hands too, illuminating his furious face. A second shifter emerges and attempts to jump Rowan, and the fire leaps from Rowan's hand, immediately forming a burning circle around his assailant. The hulking guy swears and freezes—or as frozen as you can be around fire.

"Quite the team." Viggo moves from the dark too but doesn't approach, crossing his arms over his chest instead. Sure, impressive, and inhumanly large muscles bulge, but Viggo must know not to mess with me by now. The first shifter learned because he's sensibly not retaliating.

"Well, isn't this a pleasant surprise," I say evenly.

"I know this fucker helped you at the memorial. Did he help you kill Rory and the human kid too?" Viggo spits out. "You pair now prowling around for another victim?"

"You're inebriated and tiresome," I inform him. "And pointlessly set your dogs on us. Or are they wolves? Bears?"

"Everybody in town knows your asshole father is protecting you. Someone needs to deal with his little girl."

"Again, drunk and tiresome, plus a little stupid." I flick the flames on my fingers in a bored fashion and Rowan stands side by side with me, fire in his hand at the ready too. "A *lot* stupid if you refuse to learn."

"Somebody also needs to teach you a lesson." Viggo takes a step closer and then staggers back as a flaming circle to match his friend's appears around him. "Fuck!" He dances around and whacks at the flames licking his boots, and I fight laughing.

"Don't. Touch. Her," snarls Rowan.

"Or what?" Viggo sneers.

"Rowan," I warn as he steps forward.

"Or Rory won't be the only dead shifter."

Deadly magic surges across the bond, and my chest goes tight. He's *serious*. "Rowan, no."

"Hey. Guys. Hear that. The Blackwood's sidekick threatened us." He jerks his chin. "Killed to impress her, huh? Sicko."

"Rowan. You have no reason to protect me," I say and snatch his arm. A jolt as intense as the first time we touched blinds me, and I stagger—this is a thousandfold stronger than by the fire at the gathering. "Stop before this gets worse."

"I don't fucking care!" he shouts, and I take a sharp breath when the steel eyes meeting mine are tinged with shadow.

I'm fueling this.

Rowan wrenches from my grip and strides towards Viggo's fire circle before pausing. Viggo snarls at Rowan, unable to cross the meter high flames, but as Rowan jerks his chin, he gasps and grips his chest. Viggo's face twists with pain before he lands on his knees, centimeters from the fire.

The flames surrounding Rowan's original attacker drop away as the witch refocuses his magic, and the guy charges into the night after the other who already ran. If they're sensible, the guys won't return with more shifters.

As Rowan steps to the very edge of the flames and looks down at Viggo, the magic drifts around him like clouds. No—not clouds. Shadow.

Oh, no. *No.* Blackwood. "You say I'm stupid?" I shout at Rowan. "Stopping a shifter's heart? That's insanity."

"Just a warning not to underestimate us. And not to touch you," growls Rowan.

"Stopping non-immortals' hearts ends their lives, Rowan."

Rowan's low laugh lifts hairs on the back of my neck. Since the night I discovered our bond, I've hidden, self-absorbed by the effect on me, worried that my unshackled emotional responses would lead to trouble.

I never thought my effect on Rowan could threaten his and the world's safety too.

Chapter Ten

VIOLET

Viggo continues to clutch his chest, doubling over as he sways, and even through the dim, the Blackwood shadows hover around Rowan, barely visible but there.

Nobody but Dorian and I can practice Blackwood magic, and the Blackwood shadows that witches unleashed in the past are now caged and inaccessible so none could ever succumb to them again. Rowan took on Blackwood energy when our souls converged, and the shifters' actions tonight sparked the need to protect his witch bond. Somehow, Rowan connected with the worst of my family's magic—the shadows.

"Rowan! Stop!" I yell as the shadows begin to engulf the pair.

My heart races as Viggo's slows. If Rowan reacts this way when somebody threatens me, what the hell will he do if anybody ever manages to hurt me?

I batter my mind against Rowan's, trying to take hold of the shadows but meet a solid black wall. He's pure witch and so more potent than my half-witch, even before I gave him more magic. The only way to stop his actions is to tune into my vampiric strength, and I prepare to attack.

A figure practically flies from the direction the shifters came from, heading straight for Rowan. Rowan's spell grip on Viggo drops as the newcomer slams into Rowan and seizes hold. Moments later, Rowan's hauled away but by someone different to a shifter. A familiar scent.

Leif.

I sprint after them into the gloom. A few hundred meters away, Leif holds Rowan against a wide trunk, hands digging into his shoulders as the two stare at each other through the dim. The shadows aren't around Rowan now and although his chest continues to heave, he isn't fighting Leif.

"Rowan. Listen to me. You don't do this shit." Leif grabs his face and holds so Rowan's gaze has to remain on his. "What the fuck got into you?"

"Me." I reach the pair, mesmerized by Leif's effect on Rowan. How? This witch successfully blocked me out moments ago.

"Huh?" Leif looks between us. "You taught him dark magic?"

"No. He's...." I trail off.

Rowan pulls his face from Leif's hand and meets my furious eyes. "We're bonded," he says, not looking back to Leif.

"Whoa." Leif's grip on Rowan slackens. "I guess you got two things you wanted, Rowan."

"What does that mean?"

Leif glances over. "Power, and you."

"Rowan does not have me," I retort. "This bond is merely an inconvenience for us both and certainly not one I'll pursue. Look at what this has done to him. And you've no idea what the bond has done to *me*."

"Calm down." He looks back to his friend. "Will *you* calm down or do you need me to shut you up?"

"Shut Rowan up?"

"We have an agreement. I calm Rowan if he goes too far, to keep him out of trouble."

"Calm, how?" I ask.

"Dunno. Maybe the threat of my fist in his face works?" replies Leif.

Do all these guys have masochistic tendencies—look at Grayson and his casual 'somebody hit me'. "Controlling Blackwood magic won't be easy now he's succumbed, Leif. Rowan almost stopped Viggo's heart."

Leif gapes at his friend. "What? Are you a fucking idiot, Rowan?"

"He attacked us. Wanted to hurt Violet," Rowan says through gritted teeth.

"If you ever do something that stupid to pointlessly come to my defense again, I'll—"

"You'll what? Break off our relationship?" Rowan coughs out a laugh.

Shoving Leif out of the way, I stand in front of Rowan and look up. The Blackwood energy still hovers around him, less tangible, but present and stroking at my mind too. I constantly avoid meeting Rowan's eyes because the reflection of myself they contain disturbs me. Standing close to him unsettles me too because Rowan's attraction becomes clearer each time. But now he's a tightly wound tangle of anger and frustration instead.

"You're lucky I held back from protecting you," I grit out. "Because if I'd hurt one of the shifters, I'd be arrested and back in the detectives' firing line."

"You would've *protected* me?"

"Good grief!" I step back. "We're bonded. I don't want you, but I can't help what this evokes in me."

"Charming as ever, Violet," he retorts.

"I never understood the bonded witch thing," says Leif. "Is this like mates?"

"Like shifter mates?" I ask in horror. "I'm not mating with Rowan!"

Leif's snorted laugh riles me further. "No. Like, fated."

I bite back more anger. "Unfortunately, yes. I'm hoping that my hybrid status weakens the bond."

Rowan grumbles and straightens his ruffled blazer as he moves from the tree. "You instinctively attacked someone who hurt me, Violet. Good luck with weakening the bond."

"Hey, at least Rowan's your bonded witch," says Leif lightly, looking between where we shoot poisonous looks at each other. "He knows and accepts who you are. Could be worse."

How could this be worse? Whatever danger the bond opened in me that risks others' safety, I've also triggered an extreme magical reaction in a witch who once told me he craves power.

Why am I still shaking? Our eyes remain locked, and the intensity snatches my breath. "Why were you lurking in the woods, Leif?" I ask, cutting Rowan dead before he can get words from his open mouth.

"I wasn't. I saw what was happening from the sidewalk." He shakes his head. "I'm not sure if anyone else saw, but I'm betting the guys will report you."

"Oh, yes. Especially Rowan's clear death threat," I snipe.

"Why are you walking around town?" asks Rowan, and I seethe as he ignores me. "We were coming to the house."

"Yeah, but you mentioned Viggo was on the warpath, and I worried he'd find me. Shifter elders contacted Marlene, looking for me, and I left her house before anything could happen. I don't want her under threat too." He pulls a face at Rowan. "I told you I should've left town."

"Staying away from Thornwood isn't a great plan, Leif." Rowan's stance and manner move back towards normal, the darkness filtering away. "Come back tonight."

Leif digs hands into his hoodie pockets and glances in the

direction he found us. "Yeah. I'm not leaving campus again until Viggo and his mates calm down about Rory's murder."

"And you'll explain to me what's happening with you?" I ask. "What scares you this much about Viggo? He's just a kid's brain in an overgrown body."

"The issue is more than Viggo, Violet." He yanks his hood up and partially obscures his face. "Have you crossed me off your suspect list?"

"You're not on any list," I reply. *Any longer.*

"Right. If you trust me and I can trust you, we'll talk." The edginess has returned. Leif's guardedness—how did I never notice that he deflects from himself by talking about Rowan whenever we speak? Leif hid from me as much as I've hidden from him.

"Tonight?"

"Tomorrow," he says firmly. "One of us needs to keep an eye on Rowan. He takes a while to snap out of it when he's fired up like this."

Rowan was bad *before* we bonded?

The witch huffs and rests against the trunk but doesn't protest. "Fine. Leave. The bastards spoiled our date, anyway."

"Date?" Leif looks between us. "Is *that* why you and Rowan are together? Weird. Did you have fun?"

"I buried Wesley's toe, and Rowan blackmailed me into eating dinner with him. Not a romantic rendezvous."

"Sounds like your kind of date, Violet." Leif chuckles and hauls Rowan forward by his torn blazer. "Come with me, you moron."

"Where?" asks Rowan.

"Back to the academy before you kill someone."

A week ago, I'd presume Leif's words were for me.

But they're not.

Chapter Eleven

VIOLET

I'VE AN INSANE AMOUNT TO UNPACK FROM YESTERDAY. A simple day snooping at a funeral and a sneaky toe burial became something unimaginable. Mind whirling with thoughts and theories—and focused on avoiding Rowan—I walked away from the pair once we reached campus last night.

Rowan and Leif have an unusual relationship. I don't sense anything beyond a close friendship, although there's a hint of mutual dependence. Such closeness with another should help balance the bond a little, although it's almost as if they come as a 'pair'.

Leif agrees to meet me at lunch, and I stress to him this meeting would be without Rowan. He's one of the things that needs unpacking, but I doubt I'll discover anywhere to neatly put him away. I wasn't joking about my coming to Rowan's defense—if we're compelled to protect each other like last night, we're dangerous to ourselves as much as others.

Why am I losing control at the time I most need it?

The complexity surrounding the crimes makes using a notepad cumbersome, and I rip pages out and attach them to the wall beside the window with sticky tape. One page per theory. Suspect lists. More.

If the murderer intends to frame me and bring trouble for Dorian, I'm at a loss who's responsible. Viggo's comments about my father last night held a hint that he's more aware of Dorian's role than I expected. But a shifter murdering one of his own?

Which brings me to my second theory based on Kai's words. *Pulling Rory into line.* But again, why? At the memorial, Rory seemed very much on Viggo's side—a right-hand man happy to take on the hybrid girl. Or was that the ploy—the shifters wanted me to threaten one of them and create a new potential victim?

I rub my temples. That seems a little too mastermind for the thick-headed creatures I've encountered. And what about the rune? Somebody else at the memorial used my fight with Rory to select a new 'Violet victim'?

Listing attendees takes up two sheets of paper alone. Students. Teachers. Town dignitaries. Kai's father attended—with the number of people present, I hadn't noticed or paid much attention to him. At the time, Sawyer was merely one amongst several of the town council.

Is Sawyer involved? Kai? One thing's sure, I need to look into his business and the conflict with shifters over land. I add more notes onto one of the papers attached to the wall, connect people with drawn arrows, and write a timeline of events.

Even if I weren't a suspect, I'm compelled to do this. I hate when things are out of natural order and prefer life simple and predictable—another reason I've always resisted my parents' attempts to integrate me into the world.

I've a keen mind but this entangled mess of lives within and outside of the town and academy will take some unpicking. I scrawl a circle in the middle with a question mark. What's the missing link between all three? Who's closely connected to Dorian's council and who's opposed? Because both types will live around the academy and town. My father has supporters and enemies in equal measure. Well, mostly equal, I expect it's skewed against him.

Tapping my pen on my teeth, I admire my handiwork, already plotting my next move. Holly arrives at the room with a bag of chips in her hands. Expecting her to hop straight onto the bed and open both the bag and laptop, I say hello and then continue with my musing.

No bed creak, rustle, or Netflix sound.

"What's that?" she asks and crosses to examine the papers now taking up a large expanse of the white-painted wall.

"My findings and theories." I smile, rather proud of my work.

Blowing air into her cheeks, Holly peruses the papers. "I can hardly decipher your writing, Violet. This is all a bit... chaotic."

"As is the situation."

"What's that page with the list of names? Your main suspects?" She steps forward to take a closer look.

My predicted future victims who I'll need to avoid clashing with. But tell Holly that? No.

"Viggo, I understand. Kai not so much." The chip bag crunches in her hand. "And Mr. Willis?" She gawks. "You think he killed his own son? You're insane."

I give a tight smile.

"Huh. Still don't trust the guys?" She taps the paper where I've written their three names. "I'm glad I'm not on the list."

"As am I." I turn away and place my pen into a desk drawer.

"Will you be around today? Or are you seeing your other friends?"

"You're my only friend, Holly. The guys are..." What? How do I classify the three? I still haven't told her about the bond since denial stopped me. "Acquaintances?" I suggest.

She smiles. "I'm the only person promoted to friend status? Such an honor."

Too much talking. I grab my boots from by the bed. Holly's mouth turns down. "I'd hoped you were free."

I slant my head. Odd. "Why? This isn't another attempt at a girls' afternoon, is it? Plans to watch more shows that give me nightmares?"

"Give you nightmares about what?"

"I had flashbacks all day. About the ick."

"Do you mean the sex scenes?"

"Stop right there." I hold a hand up. "Don't trigger the images again."

"You're oddly prudish, Violet."

"Frankly, I'm shocked. Why on earth would you force me to watch pornography?" I grimace. "The kissing was bad enough, but I sat through that part because you wanted company. And then the sex? I wish I hadn't."

"It's not just porn. There is a story. They're in love."

I snort. "Everything about their 'love' is gross."

"Have you ever kissed someone, Violet?" Stunned she'd ask such a thing, I don't respond. Her eyes go wide. "You *haven't*. Aren't you curious to try?"

"Why? Do you want to kiss me because we're friends now?" I'm increasingly confused. "Is that part of the 'being friends'?"

Holly splutters a laugh. "Not that type of kissing for this kind of friendship. Hugging, yes."

"You want to hug me?" Every muscle in my body goes rigid.

"What is with you and physical contact, Violet?" She bites her lip. "Did something happen? Or is this just 'you'?"

"I can't keep the distance I need from others if I touch

them," I reply. "And please, no words about needing to change. It's safer this way."

Her eyes widen. "You're worried you'll attack?"

Safer for me, therefore the world. And especially Grayson. I shrug on my black jacket. "Enjoy your show. I'm late for my meeting."

"Nice conversation change, Violet. Are you meeting Rowan?"

"Leif."

"Oh. That's good." She perches on the edge of her bed. "He's a nicer guy than Rowan."

"And Rowan's best friend," I remind her.

"And another acquaintance? You're changing."

"Yes." I focus hard on the door and keep my expression guarded. "Unfortunately."

"Your changes are good for you, Violet. If you ever want to chat about anything, I'm here."

I pivot to face the girl who will always be my opposite—open, friendly, and genuinely cares about everybody she comes across. "Now you sound like my mother."

"I saw your parents the other day." She places the chips on her bed. "Your mom is beautiful. Dorian doesn't look old enough to be your dad, and he's scary."

"You're sensible to be scared of Dorian, but don't worry, he won't hurt you. Not unless you cross him."

"Like accusing you of the murders?"

"Or forcing me to do your bidding against my wishes." I sigh at her puzzled look. "Forcing me to the dance."

Holly presses her lips together. "I am not. You should meet the committee sometime; you'll see we're not empty-headed girls but people who like to help with school unity."

"With streamers and balloons?"

She glares again. "I'm learning to understand you, Violet, and that's plain rude and judgmental."

I blink. Am I transparent now too? "Then you understand what to expect from my behavior."

She straightens and walks over to me. "I've no idea how those guys put up with your unpleasantness."

Good grief. This went south quickly. All because I don't want to watch her perverse show? "Neither do I."

Snatching my phone, I then shove it in my pocket. As I reach the door, I pause. "I apologize, Holly."

Which part for? I don't know. Hopefully the part that upset her the most.

Chapter Twelve

LEIF

I'M WARY OF VIOLET. DESPITE WHAT SHE SAYS ABOUT HOW plain speaking she is, the girl's a closed book. I have seen her less uptight when alone with Holly recently and thought she might be softening. Until I saw how she interacted with Rowan last night—they're no calmer together.

The tension between the pair always held an edge that amused me because Violet and Rowan have some similarities. This bond seems to turn these similarities in polar opposite directions, repelling the pair instead of snapping them together.

Oh, man, is Rowan upset. Once he'd calmed down and stopped rambling about how he felt invincible with the Blackwood magic, he became quieter than he usually is after an uncontrolled magic incident. I attempted to ask questions about the bond with Violet and if this had changed anything apart from intensifying his magical power, but he claimed he was too tired and asked me to leave.

But I've known him since our first day at the academy and

we walked together along the rocky teenage path, past the bullies and confusion, to an understanding and loyalty that's unbreakable. He's the closest I have to a brother and through that closeness I know him well. So, it's clear to me that Violet's attitude to the bond has sliced through the guy's guarded heart.

Rowan's growing obsession with Violet before the bond revelation concerned me because he often retaliates against people who annoy him. That clash would not end well for him if directed at Violet Blackwood. Then one day it hit me —Rowan's attracted to the girl he took delight in poking, in the hope she'd bite, one way or another.

I don't know a lot about witches and how their society works, or what these bonds mean, but if the bond heightened Rowan's mental and emotional fragility, and he now craves Violet more, I'm concerned. Now, this clashing energy between Rowan and Violet gathers momentum, feeding their intense magic. They're a dry thunderstorm ready to strike and one day ignite the world and each other.

Violet's not wearing the uniform, which makes her even easier to spot as she purposefully strides across the lawn towards me. I understand Rowan's attraction because there's something about Violet that's wormed into my heart and mind too. A 'something' that prompted me to interfere in her fight with the shifters at the memorial. I can't lose the unnecessary need to protect the slender, pretty girl, or the desire to make her perpetually dour face light up and smile at me.

That isn't happening now—Violet greets me with a scowl. Her baggy black cardigan almost reaches the ground and I'm distracted that her legs are more visible thanks to the short skirt over black leggings.

"This is hardly the weather for sitting in the middle of a field," she informs me. "Why couldn't we meet inside?"

I frown at the cloudless spring sky. "I don't see rain anytime soon."

"The sun hurts my eyes." Violet squints as if to confirm the pain.

"I didn't think the sun burned vamps any longer? Or that it ever bothered hybrids."

"I burn easily."

"You seemed fine when you put out the flames in art class with your hand." I grin at her as she presses her lips together, clearly unamused. I lean back, propping myself up by placing my palms on the ground behind. "If you want to hear my story, we're staying here."

Violet flicks her tongue against her top teeth. "Why do you guys always want to control the situation?"

"I don't. I'm enjoying the spring day before the weather you prefer returns." And teasing, knowing she won't walk away. "You're the one trying to control the situation by telling me to leave."

"You've evidently taken lessons from Rowan." She sits and draws her knees to her chest, slender fingers linked around them. The warmth tinges her cheeks pink, an unusual difference that she wouldn't have as a vamp.

All vampires are beautiful. Straight statement—they're created this way to dazzle and overwhelm. But their beauty comes with an edge to the perfection, their stone-carved features not entirely human looking, despite sensual mouths and captivating eyes.

Violet's mother gifted her looks that smooth the edge away, leaving Violet with a face as mesmerizing as any vampire but as pretty as a human girl. And those eyes. Since I met Violet, I'm finally aware how her father managed to charm his way into the position he holds, then dig his claws firmly in the top spot once he took it. Why hasn't Dorian taught Violet to use her looks and some of his subtle mind tricks rather than teach her to close off what she could be?

Maybe Dorian tried and she refused. Whatever, this girl doesn't need soft eyes and a softer smile to reel me in or use her mental magic skills—I'm enthralled.

"I apologize for teasing you," I say and mimic her position. "I've been stuck in a house hiding for a few days and so wanted some fresh air."

Violet blinks. "Sorry?"

I shake my head and smile at how Violet uses the word as if it's expected and only for certain people. "Have you spoken to Rowan yet?"

"I haven't found time. I wanted to speak to you first."

"Rowan's a mess, Violet."

"That's an unkind thing for a friend to say. I'd never expect you to judge by appearances." Is she serious? Because she has the Violet deadpan thing going on. "And to be frank, you're not exactly well-groomed yourself."

"No," I chuckle. "Mentally." Emotionally. "Can you be kinder to Rowan?"

"Aren't we here to talk about you?" she asks stiffly. *Sorry, Rowan. I tried.* "What's threatening you more than Viggo? A friend told me that the shifter elders aren't kind to half-shifters."

"A friend." I mock gasp. "Who is this mythical creature?"

"Acquaintance," she corrects. "Holly is my only friend."

"I might be insulted by that," I suggest.

Violet tips her head. "You're friendly, but not a friend."

Wow. "Then why care about what happens to me?" A muscle in her cheek twitches, a sign that Violet's holding back words; something she never did in the past. "Yeah, I know. I'm important for your investigation," I add flatly.

"I wouldn't like you falsely accused. That's why I'm gathering every fact I can from you to solve the crimes. Then we can go our separate ways."

Nothing changes. No wonder Rowan struggles with her. "Will you help me leave one day?"

Again, silence. "Yes, but you can't come with me."

Irritation prickles at Violet's immediate dismissal. "I never asked that. I'm sure you're way too important for me."

"Probably. Please, tell me your story and I can help."

"Help?" I choke a laugh. "Help yourself."

Violet turns her head away and her linked fingers squeeze around her knees until they go white. "I'm dealing with a lot, Leif."

"Yeah, the witch bond. The murder accusations. Stuck on a lawn with a half-shifter in the sun."

"I'm not myself due to several situations," she continues, her face shuttered as she looks at me. "But I will be her again. If this makes me single-minded and rude as I strive to achieve that, so be it. I am learning about people, but that does not change my general and clearly spoken contempt for most."

"Right. Understood." Man, she's funny.

"Good. Go ahead with your story." She pauses. "Please?"

I chuckle. "Learning pleasantries, huh?" She arches a brow. "Okay. I'm frightened of shifter elders. Or more precisely, my father's old elders before he left to marry Mom. These elders are forcibly taking back any who've left the community—and their kids." She looks at me, silent, unnerving. "But I'm more human than shifter; I don't ever want to shift. I'm terrified my human side will interfere and I'll become a mid if I'm provoked."

"At least the shifters wouldn't attempt to take you if that happens," she puts in. "Elders still hate mids." My jaw drops at her insensitivity. "I detect I said something wrong?"

"Violet. I want to remain human. A mid would be worse than being a shifter." I pause as her energy darkens. "I'm not prejudiced against mids; I know one of your fathers is one. Life's complicated enough for me, that's all."

"Can't your father tell the elders you're not interested? He left the community if he married your mother."

I swallow. "Dad died when I was a kid. Mom never told

me the whole story, but I swear the elders were involved. I'm worried that if I don't do what they want, I'll die too."

Violet falls quiet and pulls at a daisy she's plucked from the ground, methodically removing petals, lost again. Her silence drags by and I'm about to stand and walk away, hurt at her reaction, but Violet looks up.

"One of my fathers could help—Ethan or Zeke. They both work on keeping the peace within the shifter community and would expect me to mention your problem."

"Zeke's from the Tigris community originally, right?" She nods. "And Tigris don't communicate with the outside world or want to integrate into human society."

"Are you part Tigris?" She flicks a look at my covered body and then to my bare arms. "I saw your chest. You don't have stripes. Zeke does."

"Like I said, more human than shifter."

"I wanted stripes as a kid. Drew them on. I stuck tiny stickers that I colored black too, so that I had scales like my other dad." She smiles at me. "Stripes aren't that bad."

Violet *smiled*. That smile reaches into my chest and squeezes my heart, and the irritation with her clueless response disappears. If Violet knew her response brightened the sunny day further, she'd hate it.

"Are you alright?" she asks. "You look like you're in pain."

"Omigod." I stifle a laugh. "Fine. Well, not fine, since I'm worried for my safety."

She nods. "Tigris are particularly bad; they terrorized Zeke." *Great, that information helps. Not.* "That's why he works to help others. I'll introduce you. Zeke can help."

I snort. "By giving me a bodyguard?"

"You can't give up," she says. "Don't surrender to bullies. If there's one thing you know I won't accept, it's bullies."

"One of many things you won't accept, Violet?"

"Correct."

I shake my head at her. "That's why I'm at Thornwood—

shifters have nothing to do with the place—but I'm worried that'll change with all this upheaval. If I don't permanently get away, they'll take me. That's why I was at Marlene's. She's Mom's friend and a halfway house while I decided whether to risk running."

"And you asked for my help that day because I could get you further, quicker?" she asks curiously.

I push curls from my face. "Yeah. These murders... I don't know what's happening between shifters and other supes, but it's getting worse and not just for me. I feel like whoever is doing this wants a bigger wedge between races in our community. The two deaths weren't personal. How could they be? The two guys are from two different worlds."

She plucks another daisy. "Who do you think killed Wesley and Rory?"

"I don't know but will do everything I can to help you unravel this. If prejudice grows against shifters, I'll be targeted by kids at the academy. Sometimes I think the elders are waiting for me to shift. Wanting something to provoke me."

"So that they can take you back?"

"Yeah. You know shifters have a separate jurisdiction. Dorian's council would need to hand me to them." He moistens his lips. "What if the murders were supposed to implicate me, not you? Or to provoke me into defending myself? The scratch marks reported on the bodies were big enough to be a shifter's."

"You were questioned. You're not a suspect. The runes point to me or a witch." She rubs a cheek. "Unfortunately."

"You've dropped your 'Rowan mind-controlled Leif' theory?"

"Now I have more facts and a small window into Rowan's thoughts, yes."

"You can read his thoughts?" I gape. "That would make him pissed. He's a secretive guy."

"No. I can't read his mind, but I'm more in tune with how

he feels, which is a new experience for me. And how pissed do you think *I* am?" She clenches her teeth. "The way he behaved last night, Leif. He triggered me too—to protect him. I'm trying to protect *myself* from a murder charge, Leif, and I don't want a true one. You ask me why I'm unkind and avoid Rowan? Because our bond might trigger something horrendous inside me or encourage his darker magic. And then..." She waves a hand. "Then I truly am fucked."

Chapter Thirteen

LEIF

FUCKED. I'VE NEVER EVER HEARD THAT WORD FROM VIOLET, nor seen her cool slip like this.

"I'll help, Violet. I've influence over Rowan. Last night I struggled, but I calmed him eventually."

"How do you? You've no magic." Her mouth parts. "Wait. Do you know that's a Tigris trait? Zeke's a full-blooded shifter and he can also heal. Your effect on Rowan must be part of that side of you. Do you call on the spirits? Zeke swears they exist and help him, but I think it's his imagination."

Her words tear open a possibility I never knew existed. I'd considered fighting the animal side, but a helpful side? I've only heard about the Tigris savagery and their mindless killing when they're shifted. Dad died when I was too young to remember him well, but his choice of profession makes sense now. Dad worked at the hospital as a nurse.

"No spirits," I mumble, heart now firmly lodged in my throat. "Rowan knows I'm physically stronger. We've made an agreement that I'll restrain him if he's lost control."

"He could hurt you! Elemental magic includes fire and storm, and now he has mine."

"Rowan isn't keen on people touching him, Violet. My touch is enough to shock him out of his magical state and now it sounds like the Tigris skill helps."

Violet falls quiet. Like *she* doesn't want touch. Violet's childhood left her unable to see past people's fronts, the way she won't allow people past hers. How little does she understand Rowan?

"Can I ask you something?" she says eventually.

"Sure."

"Would you allow me to look at your memories from the night Wesley died?"

I tense. "You haven't already?"

"No." She frowns. "That's invasive. I only do so without permission if necessary."

"I can't remember from the time I left the fire up to the point I saw Rowan. There aren't any memories to see."

Violet trains a steady gaze on me. "Then how do you know you didn't kill Wesley?"

A sharp burst of annoyance rushes through me. "Another accusation, Violet?" I ask through gritted teeth.

"Merely a fact." She taps her lips. "Although memory blanks make things tricky, can I try?"

I shrug. "You won't find anything."

"You never said anything about missing memories before."

"What is there to say? A punch to the head could've caused it; you heard the nurse that day. She worried I had a concussion." And *I* worried that the scratches and extra injuries were defensive from Wes. If I hid this from myself, how could I tell others?

"If someone affected your mind with magic, I'll know." Violet kneels, hands on her knees, and looks at me expectantly.

"Are you accusing Rowan again?"

"I've an unfortunate connection to him now, remember? Rowan was not involved. I'd know—that's a huge thing to mentally hide." She rubs her hands along her leggings. "Rowan isn't the only skilled magic user—both witches and vamps can alter weak minds, especially…" She trails off and screws her face up. I can't help chuckle to myself at this new thing Violet does with her growing self-awareness, even though I know exactly what word she's suppressing.

"Shifters?"

She nods curtly. "Or humans. Especially in a state of distress."

"Why would somebody alter my mind?" I ask.

"Isn't that obvious? You saw something you shouldn't."

"Then why not kill me too? Simpler."

"Very good point, Leif. I'll make a note. Do the investigators know you have missing memories?"

"No. I lied. They're too focused on you, anyway. Probably think I'm too dumb to know how to draw a half-decent rune. I am, by the way."

"Yes. I expect you are. But can I look inside your mind?"

I smile, itching to brush the hair from Violet's face so I can see her eyes better. She's never sat this close to me before —even in class that day she shifted far away, and she smells sweeter than I imagined. An alluring vampire scent?

"Do you need to touch me?" I ask.

"Certainly not," she says with an unnecessary amount of revulsion to her tone. "If I wanted to, I'd read you across a room."

"Okay. Go ahead," I say flatly. "Permission granted."

How did I expect Violet's mental invasion to feel? I've a natural protective response to pull myself out of the wooziness caused, but I lace my fingers together and squeeze. Violet isn't the first to get into my head, but few have. Rowan always respects my refusal, since he dislikes people seeing too much of his self.

The witch detectives rummaged around but couldn't find anything. Maybe a concussion did cause the memory loss?

Violet performs her spell in silence, eyes closed and a steady calmness around her aura. I take the chance to look at her closely, then stop in case she encounters the unclean thoughts that leads to.

"Interesting," she says as she opens her eyes.

"Did you see something?" My pulse rate ticks up—I *want* Violet to see, but I'm scared of *what*.

Violet shakes her head, brow creased. "No. The magic in your mind splintered your memories into tiny pieces. Your recollections are like a 5000 piece jigsaw puzzle; I'd barely find anything, even if I stayed in your mind for an hour."

"Is that magic common?"

She lifts her eyes to mine. "No, Leif, but if I can see the memories exist, then you might gradually piece them together. That's a positive."

I bloody hope so. I'd theorized I'd forgotten due to trauma, but this confirms someone messed with my mind. The worry remains—what if I remember something bad I did that night and I don't *want* to share? "The headache you just gave me isn't so positive," I say and smile.

"Oh. Was I a bit too rough with you?" And I'm pissed with myself that those words conjure up something way more than 'rough' mind reading. I'm more obsessed by this girl than I realized. "I can tell. Your face is weird again."

Crap. I'm a heartbeat away from saying something about how I feel but smile instead. Violet's trust in me comes from respecting her boundaries. "I'll head back to my room and take a rest before class."

She shields her eyes against the sun and looks up at me when I stand. "I'm glad you came back to the academy. I want you here."

My heart skips. "Yeah?"

"Yes. I think you have answers I need."

Typical Violet. Whatever she says about her new 'emotions', she's as subtle as a large, painful brick.

Last night, Rowan rambled about how Violet's softening to him. I'd call him delusional. There's nothing soft about the hybrid girl, and I hope he accepts he might never wear her down.

Chapter Fourteen

ROWAN

LIKE MEETS LIKE.

I didn't know how accurate those words to Violet were the first day we met in the library. But there's a major difference that's now an issue—my self-control is shot.

I've never possessed that skill, which made friendships tricky. I react in extreme ways to an argument, and towards anyone who upsets my friends. Hence, I've few. My reputation as the weird, skinny kid when I first arrived grew through my years here, and nowadays most kids avoid me. I've always had an affinity with Leif since he was 'the weird kid' for other reasons and as the years passed, we've kept an eye on each other.

Nowadays, I'm more interested in learning superior magic than anything else in my life, and that keeps me away from most people.

Or that *was* my only goal.

Violet, the epitome of cool, distant, and uber-controlled, exploded my world in a way I'd never imagine. This new force created by the bond forces me to ensure she's safe and has cut the thin ties to my self-control, even though I'm perfectly aware she doesn't need my help. Violet whines that I've unlocked the gate to her emotions and that could cause problems, but she's only one half of this bond.

We triggered each other. Whatever this connection unleashes in Violet, I'll absorb too, and the bond strengthens dangerous parts of me.

Hell, if Viggo had touched Violet last night, I would've struck first and sucked up consequences later. Would I have killed the guy? Unlikely, but not impossible. The darkness from the Blackwood magic I've sought my whole life gripped me. If anybody manages to harm Violet, I can't guarantee I'd let them live.

A couple of years ago, after Wesley gave me a black eye, my rage and potent magic started a fire in Darwin House. Luckily for all occupants, me and Leif discovered he can calm me down and we put out the fire. Leif's unsure why he has that effect. Probably a shifter trait—but we don't mention the 's' word.

But Leif can't be around me 24/7, so he isn't always there when my brain flips and the magic takes over. Like the day he stopped me as I terrified Wes into almost jumping from the academy roof. Oh, I wouldn't have made Wes jump; I'd planned more unpleasant things to do to him. Things that don't leave visible scars.

I'm careful. I can't risk expulsion when Thornwood is the best place to fine tune my abilities. Good thing Wes didn't want anybody to know what happened that day. Only Leif knows.

The desire for unparalleled magic energy isn't the only thing the bond with Violet creates. Even before this happened, I'd become captivated by the dark-hearted girl. Initially, because our verbal sparring drew me in, and because I loved seeing the angry spark in her beautiful blue eyes, but the more time I spent around Violet, the more I noticed other things.

How gracefully she moves, the curves she often hides beneath her baggier clothes. I can't stop staring at her lips or obsessing about what I didn't see beneath the towel the night in her room. The image of what I did see won't leave—the softer faced, more vulnerable looking girl who was anything but when she attacked. That was the moment she moved from worthy adversary to the girl I wanted to *notice* me.

I sit in the library with my laptop and books and ignoring class, but fight to concentrate because I'm engulfed by Violet, even without her here. I knew about Kai's father, but hadn't considered a connection. He seemed too distant from the situation, plus he's on the council, so any disruption and fears for town safety won't help him keep his position of trust.

There's no doubt the wealthy and influential Sawyer keeps that position for his own purposes, and his history needs investigating.

I trawl the internet, then locate and examine the website for Sawyer Industries, a site that's aimed at trading partners, not customers. I read a brief bio singing Sawyer's praises that also lists his awards for business excellency. Digging deeper, I find town council meeting minutes, but he's held his position for ten years—running through all those will take more than a morning's work.

There're also news stories about the generous donations to the town, particularly the school where there's a scholarship he created. One named after himself; in case anybody dare forget what a wondrous benefactor he is.

Christopher Sawyer's enterprise is the center of town employment too. Quite the man.

I've never needed to pay attention to humans outside of outwitting them, and I'm surprised how similar to witch society they are, with their hierarchies and prestige from family names. A search on the Sawyer name brings up photos of the factory, and others showing him at awards ceremonies. One looks like a gala dinner, Kai's mother in an elegant blue dress beside his father in a tux, and two other couples in the row of people. They're photographed against a red velvet backdrop with the award name pinned, and the scarlet color unfortunately accentuates one couple's pale vampire skin.

I'm not *au fait* on vampire society but do know that they mix in human businesses. They always did, even before we revealed ourselves—apart from hemia who mostly survived on family inheritances. The 'not walking in the sun' made a mess of any company takeover plans, but now that they can, their influence grew tenfold. I examine the names matching the photos.

The world stops for a second.

The couple with them? Josef and Eliza Petrescu.

Heart racing, I type their names into the search bar, digging into their lives too. Josef is a partner in a prestigious law firm in the city, and names Sawyer Industries as one of his clients.

Holy crap.

I'm wrapped up in the details of the Petrescus' connections and extensive family lines, unaware of the quiet library surroundings, but Violet's presence filters into the room before I see her. My heart speeds for different reasons— how the hell do I explain last night? Have I pushed Violet further away? No doubt we're about to engage in some mutual tongue lashing and not the kind I'd like.

Well, I have new information to distract her with should she start sniping at me.

Violet pauses opposite of the desk, the one I've chosen in our unofficial meeting place, and I look up. She's wearing the academy uniform, and I know she hates the clothes as much as I do, so she must've come from class. The black and yellow could blend her in with similar looking girls if you stood behind her, but she's unmistakable should you see her face.

I've never met Dorian or Eloise, but they must be stunning to create a child like Violet. Even with her dark aura, that beauty distracts people—a dark-haired image of Dorian, I expect. He uses his looks and charms deliberately; Violet has no idea how stunning she is.

And to me, bonded to the girl, she's a goddess. I smile to myself—a dark Eldritch goddess.

"Are you in a trance?" she asks.

I can't help laughing at her. "Not quite."

She nods at the books. "Is one of those your precious grimoire?"

"Yeah. If you're nice to me, I'll let you take a look." Oh, how wonderful that first meeting was. Did an unknown part of me know what we were then?

"If you want me to help with your secret spell, I'll need to, won't I?" she retorts.

Here we go again... "You're a ray of sunshine this morning, sweet Violet."

A sharp spike of her pissed energy hits me. "I don't know what you're smirking at because last night's events are a serious situation."

"Didn't you enjoy our date?" Her sullen face becomes sour. "Oh? Are we finally going to discuss the effect of the bond?" I ask with mock surprise.

Silence.

"I spoke to Leif, and he informed me that you frequently overreact." Violet crosses her arms, blazer sleeves pulling back to show her delicate wrists. "Is the bond making this behavior worse?"

"I always told you how powerful I am, Violet, and you dismissed me in your superior way. You never asked why I had so few friends and this is why." I shove hair from my face. "And, like you, I don't give a crap."

Her eyes widen. *Like you.* "I'm concerned what our bond has created in you, Rowan."

"Concerned? About me?" I ask, ensuring the sarcasm drips even though I'm seriously surprised.

"No. Concerned what you'll do. One of us off the rails is bad enough, we can't both be. How would that reflect on me?"

I sigh. "Naturally, you're not worried about *me*. And I presume you're talking about yourself as the deranged and derailed one?"

Her brow creases—frowning shouldn't look cute on Violet, but to me? Yeah. "I remain in control currently, but I suggest you don't place yourself in life-threatening situations, Rowan."

"Um. Not planning to."

"Good. Because the last thing I need is a murder charge for one I actually commit." Violet huffs again. "This horrendous bond."

"Mmm. Horrendous," I echo. "Who knew such an atrocity could befall us?"

Her kissable mouth purses. "I don't know whether to agree with the sentiment or ignore that as sarcasm."

I respond with a smirk because I adore how Violet's eyes flare when I annoy her—and my smirking guarantees the response. Unsure if this conversation will continue, I look back to my laptop.

"What are you doing?" she asks after a few moments.

"Research. After all, I am your deputy." I look up again. "And I've discovered something very interesting."

The way to Violet's heart—facts.

"About Rory?"

"Kai's father." I turn the laptop to face her, showing Violet the photo on the screen. "Guess who his attorney is?"

She gives me one of her disparaging looks. "If I were to play that game, I'd stand here all day. How could I possibly know?"

"Josef Petrescu."

Another of my other favorite things in life currently—squashing Violet's superior attitude "Petrescu? Is he closely related to Grayson?"

I shrug. "Vampires don't share much about themselves online. You'll need to ask him."

"Oh, I will." She purses her lips. "This interests me. Kai's family has links with vampires. Vampires and shifters clash. Shifters and the Sawyers clash. Some Petrescus refuse to support Dorian. There's a link in there."

"But how? Why kill Rory and Wesley?"

"To cause trouble for me, but maybe something else at a deeper level." I can practically hear her brain whirring, and Violet's brain processes things faster than anyone I've met, including myself. "The killer wants trouble between the town and shifters. Or the town and academy. Between Dorian's council and all. Or..." She presses a palm against her forehead. "I need to think about this. Talk to Grayson."

"Okay, but can we discuss the other thing?" I ask and place a hand on the book. "Isn't that why you're here?"

"The spell or your magically psychotic episode?" Her phone's already out of her pocket as she shifts focus. "That can wait."

"What?" I stand and point at the phone. "No. That can wait."

"Rowan. Nothing is more important than the murders." Violet's striking blue eyes meet mine and I want to shout at her, 'This is. We are. You are,' but I swallow down the words that catch in my throat. "I don't have time for this right now. I'll speak to you later," she continues, oblivious.

"Tonight?" I ask tersely.

"Only if I've spoken to Grayson. If not, we'll speak tomorrow." She tucks the phone into her pocket again.

"For fuck's sake, Violet," I grit out. "I wish I hadn't told you about the Sawyer connection."

Why am I the only one affected? Is she incapable of empathy? Feeling?

We have a fucking bond.

Apparently deaf to my words, Violet's mouth parts as it does when a thought hits. "Take me to the party with you."

"Huh?"

"Kai's party. He invited me. I'd like to look around his house."

"To steal something?"

"Borrow."

"I won't get involved this time," I say stiffly. "And I wouldn't trust you."

Momentarily, her eyes widen. "You won't take me to the party?"

How petty can I be? Because I'm pretty bloody petty when I'm pissed with someone. Especially one who's just raked her nails across my heart. Not replying, I close my laptop and shove it into my bag, then grab my books and tuck them away too.

"You, Violet Blackwood, need to crawl out of your ass and think of somebody other than yourself." I move from behind the desk.

She blows air into her cheeks. "Interesting metaphor, Rowan. I didn't say I won't talk to you about our issue and how to solve the problem. Just later."

I step closer until I'm in the space Violet keeps between her and the world; the one many instinctively avoid and give her a wide berth. "We're not a murder investigation," I say flatly. "We can't be 'solved'."

The urge to take Violet's face and tell her everything that's in my heart and head grows as I breathe in the scent and warmth from this ice cold girl. As with the other day, I catch a glimmer of something in her eyes that she blinks away.

"I am perfectly aware of that, Rowan."

I curl fingers around her hand, and the uncomfortable,

craved magic sparks between us. Hope rises in the few seconds delay before she pulls away, then the feeling drops like a stone. In that moment, I almost—almost—attempt to hug Violet, desperate to give physical comfort that she claims she doesn't need.

As if aware, Violet backs off. "I need to find Grayson."

Clutching her phone, Violet leaves, not even protesting that she wants to read my grimoire. Grayson's affecting her in some way that she can't resist, and the guy is a bloody Petrescu. I need to speak to him.

I've nothing in common with Grayson, we've never clashed or spoken much, but we certainly have a commonality now. If he hurts or threatens Violet, even indirectly, we'll more than clash.

Chapter Fifteen

VIOLET

DETERMINATION CLOUDS MY JUDGEMENT AS I SCOUR CAMPUS for Grayson. I'll deal with the attraction to his blood in the same way that I cope with Rowan's effect on me—rebuild the smashed wall between the outside world and myself.

One that threatens to collapse completely.

I'm increasingly pissed that I can't find him on campus and even go so far as attending classes I share with him. No show. Rowan is a no show too, which isn't a surprise, but I chat to Leif in a couple of classes. At least one of the three guys doesn't have a fated and possibly fateful effect on me. Although he isn't happy when I mention Grayson's name either.

By early evening, I'm torn between keeping my promise to Rowan or searching further. I'm not dumb enough to go into the woods—the day I snuck in to get close to Rory's crime scene, I was almost spotted. No visiting murder sites anymore. I'll take one last tour around the campus grounds and then I'll contact Rowan. The sooner we deal with what he wants help with, the better.

Rowan never had the chance to explain his findings fully due to my brain refocusing and overriding everything around me. Due to my growing ability to sense when I've upset people—well, Rowan and sometimes Holly—I'm aware that my meeting with him in the library triggered some of what Leif spoke about. I'm tinder to a fire that could rip through him and, as I told Rowan, that concerns me. Any time he's in danger, so am I.

I'm navigating a tightrope across a chasm between the girl I've created through my life and the girl beneath, and I'm stuck. If I'm not around Rowan and Grayson, I can pretend nothing has changed in the Violet who walked into Thornwood Academy. Stop them chipping away at that Violet to find the one they want.

I don't think they'll like what they find.

Taking my phone from my pocket, I text Rowan.

Do you want to meet now?

He doesn't respond immediately, so I stay in my room to peruse the crime wall, and add some notes about Sawyer and the vamps, grinding my teeth because I couldn't find Grayson. After half an hour lost in this, I check my phone. No reply.

Rowan?

At this point, I'm torn between worry and annoyance. *He* wanted to talk.

The decision to take the walk from Darwin House to the academy building and Rowan at Pendle House evaporates when I step into the rain. Not because I'm bothered about soaking myself on the trip between the two, but because I want to enjoy the rain.

As I child, I loved to dance naked in storms but wearing clothes in public became one social norm I adopted once my family left our exiled island. That norm certainly applies here. The beautiful, black, heavy clouds spread thickly across the sky, obliterating the moon and stars. They're here to stay.

After the few days I've had, I want the rain to wash over and remind me the world doesn't have to be chaos. Walking inside with damp, clingy clothes will be a downside, as is water puddling in my boots. Still, the clothes don't prevent the water trickling along my face, soaking my hair, and engulfing me.

Nobody else considers walking in rainstorms an attractive prospect, and the grounds are empty as I make my way through the cloisters until I'm at the other side of the academy grounds. The lawns stretch to the sports fields and close to a cottage ruined in a fire fifteen years ago. Shame, because the place would've made a great sanctuary away from the academy.

Did students once use the place for secret meetings rather than behind the greenhouse?

Greenhouse.

Yesterday, I promised Holly I'd sneak in and perk up her horticultural project. After I 'fixed' them last time, she believed the plants needed as much water as I'm enjoying now, but her generosity half-killed them again.

This is my perfect opportunity, and I splash through the puddles forming on the grass and slip through the dark towards the glass doors. The glow from my fingers soon livens the plants and I wrinkle my nose before focusing on adding budding tomatoes to them. That little extra would advance Holly's project to a grade level to match other kids.

Will I ever use my life-giving powers on anything apart from flora and fauna? Now that I'm older, surely Eloise will help me, but I understand her concern. I've assured her I'd only perform the spell on a human to help, but she replied that reanimating someone could be against their wishes and it's wrong to do so without permission.

I reminded Eloise that Dorian 'reanimated' her when she was unable to give permission, and that closed the argument down.

Do I have the ability to bring someone back from the brink with my blood? Hybrid Dorian could and did. Interesting. I'd never considered such a thing, too focused on my witch side after years suppressing the vampire.

Water drips to the floor and puddles around my feet as I finish up the task. Dragging damp hair from my face, I make my way back outside. If this were winter, the rain would be pleasurably cool and not chill me, but the spring rain holds the magic of regeneration.

A delectable new shiver trips across my skin as the sky lights up close to the edge of the academy. I never saw or sensed the electricity created by lightning in the clouds earlier, and oddly the prickling energy that heralds a storm isn't in the air around.

I wander to the edge of the greenhouse and wipe my forehead as I pause to watch for more lightning. Nothing happens for a moment until a jagged fork bolts from the sky.

Silent. No thunder. Odd.

The brief illumination from the lightning silhouettes a figure standing at the edge of the fields close to where the lightning struck. Huh. I guess some elemental witches *do* enjoy stormy weather. Although water-attuned witches can't control storms—only a few storm witches exist.

I tense. Like Rowan. Another bolt slashes the sky, and my heart jolts as if the lightning hit me as well as him. I'm too far away to see which part of him, but close enough to sense something different to pain.

Exhilaration.

Good grief, Rowan.

I stride across the field towards him. Rowan faces away, back to me, and must've been here a while as his hoodie hangs heavy with water and his jeans stick to his legs.

"Hello, sweet Violet." His tone is soft, but back still to me.

"What are you doing?" I ask.

He turns, his steel eyes almost silver with the magic, and the downpour flattens his hair, water running in rivulets down his face. "Recharging."

I glance upwards. "Conjuring electricity?"

"My best spells use storm energy. You'd know that."

"One of the most dangerous, Rowan."

"To protect myself. Us." He licks raindrops from his lips and stares at mine.

"You might kill somebody."

"Well, you can fix that." He laughs and there's a weird edge to his tone.

"Are you drunk? High?"

Rowan rubs his fingers together like kindling fire, and white sparks run across them. "Yeah. Magic gives me a high."

"Even when not under threat, a storm spell would be a bad idea. They can easily get out of control—worse than fire."

He blinks away drops from his lashes. "You've changed. A few weeks ago, you wouldn't give a crap about people getting hurt."

"You know why," I reply. "I'm not spelling this out again."

"Your so-called new emotions from the unleashed Eloise side?"

"Why say it so derisively?"

Rowan holds his arms wide either side of himself, his hoodie soaked and stretched across his chest. "You think I'm not struggling with how I feel?"

"I think you're struggling to control yourself." I gesture at the sky.

He snorts a laugh. "You have no idea."

"What? You're practicing worse spells than this? Did I see Blackwood shadow magic last night?" My panic rises: I'd hoped I imagined that. The shadows control even the most powerful witches, especially those seeking power. Rowan using Blackwood magic without me moderating him could unfetter the shadows.

Rowan drops his arms and steps closer, looking down at me, eyes still shimmering silver. He ignores my question. "If you have *feelings* now, why are frustration and anger the only emotions directed at me?" The storm energy crackles around him, spreading between us. "I feel like you blame me for something I didn't do."

Water continues to pour down his head and I'm barely aware of the relentless rain anymore. I've felt this from Rowan before and panicked, too confused to know how to help after lashing out at him.

Rowan's hurt.

"Is this about earlier?" I ask quietly. "I did agree to speak. I've looked for you to—"

"No, Violet. This is about always. From the first time I saw your pouting face and enjoyed how I triggered you. Each time I evoked any kind of response." He holds both my cheeks in his damp hands and I'm too shocked to move, oddly fascinated by the cold dampness. "I don't think it's an accident that we're bonded. Fate chose this."

"Do not create something romantic from our unwanted state. I am 'angry' and 'frustrated' around you because I don't like that I worry about you."

"*Worry?* Why?"

"You're fragile, Rowan. I am not. I could hurt you. I have spent my whole life detached so I don't hurt people and cause issues for myself. Now… this. It's confusing and annoying."

He's silent a moment, his gaze unnerving. "You freeze me out in case you hurt me? Ice can burn too, Violet."

The longer he touches me, the more his warm fingers burn through my numb cheeks and the storm magic lifts hairs on my neck and arms. In this moment as the rain soaks through, I'm aware of the connection I'm fighting—the sick feeling that I could lose control not through the bond but by *feeling* and allowing the touch my skin wants.

I'm reflected in his eyes, our magic forever entwined, and I tense as he rests his forehead on mine. "Don't push me away."

"I most certainly will if your mouth gets any closer," I say stiffly. "To the opposite end of the sports field."

He laughs, and his warm breath brushes my lips. "I know. I don't have a death wish."

I pull my head away, peel his fingers from my cheeks, and edge backwards. "An attempted kiss would upset me, but I wouldn't kill you, Rowan."

"Not literally…" He shakes his head. "Never mind."

Is the spark flowing between us still his magic? Or more? He's calmer, as if touching me soothed him despite the dark energy—although the desire in his eyes is not soothed. Neither am I as my rapid heartbeat remains, even without that touch. *Do* I want more?

"I don't need to kiss you." Rowan digs his hands into his damp jacket pockets. "You let me touch you, Violet. That response is as significant as if we'd kissed."

I stare, water running down my cheeks, where the warmth from his touch remains. "No. You're incorrect. We held hands when performing a spell."

"Ah, but this is different." He half-smiles. "Isn't it?"

"If you don't stop creating imaginary romantic exchanges, I *will* be inclined to throw you across the field."

"Interesting denial." He tips his chin. "Why are you here, then?"

"Why did you ignore my texts? You confused me because you insisted we talk and then didn't respond to me."

"Bloody hell, Violet," he says under his breath.

"What? I no longer wish to talk about…" I wave a hand. "This."

"Us?"

I flick my tongue against my teeth. "Rowan…"

He pointlessly wipes water from his face with a damp sleeve. "I ignored the texts because I was pissed with you and wanted to get the effect of that out of my system."

"The magic?"

"Yeah. You think we're different, Violet, but we're not. Strong emotion interrupts my self-control and I've a mind that holds onto and obsesses about conversations and events that upset me. If I was a shifter, I'd probably kick the crap out of people. Instead, my anger management issues channel a different way. Heightened, aggressive magic."

"I am beginning to notice."

He licks rain from his lips, a gesture that sends a weird fluttering through my chest as the magic tingles on my skin. "Kissing or no kissing, I guess we'll either control each other or be uncontrolled together."

Rowan says the words lightly, almost a joke, but there's nothing amusing here. I don't even admonish him for the kiss comment because he's hit on the truth. I'd suspected Rowan's magically more potent than he seems, and that his guarded, secretive nature had a deeper root, but there's no doubt any longer.

The witch conjured lightning and easily. He absorbed the storm energy, lit up by the magic. And he's already found my shadows. Rowan doesn't get his highs from drugs or alcohol, or even the magic. This guy thrives on the edge this gives him, and he's seeking something that could threaten our society's stability.

I know our history and what happens when power-hungry witches succumb to magic and allow darkness to take hold. The witch doesn't stop.

Dorian carefully created an illusion for the human society, one promising that supes would never threaten their world. This illusion would disappear if there's a threat and upheaval to *our* society.

The spell Rowan wants help with requires Blackwood magic—magic he's already beginning to absorb in his desire to become more powerful. Although the freezing rain has no effect on my form, I shiver.

Chapter Sixteen

VIOLET

"Don't you dare dress me up this time," I warn Holly as she selects an item from her extensive wardrobe collection. "I'm already wearing what I intend."

She turns to me and holds up the short, powder blue cardigan with pearl buttons, embroidered with darker blue and pink roses. I shudder in horror as she pulls out a matching pink and blue, short plaid skirt. If you could call plaid and floral matching. "No. This is for me to wear. Cute, right? "

I'm wearing my usual leggings and an oversize black and white striped sweater tonight, with Docs of course. I always wear my pendant and decline Holly's offer of the rings and bracelets she likes to adorn herself with.

I pull out a mirror and bag of make-up. "If Kai invites supes to parties, he isn't the one warning off kids from mixing with campus students. Must be shifters."

Holly's face takes on a harder look. "I wouldn't know. Ollie never told me."

"Kai and his friends aren't worried about threats?"

"Some. Kai isn't," she replies. "He likes academy kids, especially those who can help him against shifters."

I narrow my eyes. "Hence mine and Rowan's invite?"

She shrugs. "Possibly. I'm still surprised you decided to go to the party."

"As am I. What do you know about Kai's family?" I ask as nonchalantly as possible as I begin to draw around my eyes. "His father is a council member, but I heard the Sawyers are wealthy."

"Oh, yeah. Wait until you see their house," she exclaims. "His family even has a pool."

"A pool of what?"

Holly laughs at my apparent joke and then frowns when I remain straight-faced. "A swimming pool, Violet."

"Oh. How odd."

"Not really. Wealthy people often have them. I can't believe you don't know what a pool is. Have you never swam in one?"

"No and have no intention of such." I tense. "Is this a prerequisite for party attendees?"

"Spring weather isn't the best for swimming, but some kids will." She shivers as she pulls on her cardigan. "Not me."

"And will Kai's parents be in attendance?"

Her eyes shine as she grins. "No. His parents are in the city on business overnight."

Hmm. I'd hoped to meet the man tonight and use the party as an excuse. Now, the whole situation becomes less appealing—free-range teenagers drowning themselves in alcohol and possibly water. Although if Kai's too drunk to notice our snooping, that would help. I intend to avoid him following our encounter at the cafe and my blunt opinions.

As Holly turns away to finish her preparations, I'm on the verge of speaking to her about the funeral and my latest investigations, now that I don't believe she's feeding information to Vanessa. Apparently the woman left; either she's bad at her job or nobody wanted to speak to her. Perhaps both.

But no. Better that Holly knows only what she needs to, although she is taking an unusual interest in my investigations and unsubtly requesting daily updates. *That* needs investigating at some point too.

"Don't local humans attend Thornwood? Wesley's family isn't from town. You're not. Why isn't Kai studying here?" I hunt for my phone, which I've lost. Again.

"Because there's competition for human places at the Thornwood academies." She sits to pull her shoes on. "He either didn't try hard enough or he failed the entrance exam. Kai isn't bothered—he likes his top dog position at the local high school."

"Entrance exam? Who'd want to come here voluntarily?"

"Um. Me? You know that the highest achievers will gain positions working with supes? I'd love that."

"As long as it isn't horticultural," I say with a small smile.

"Was that a joke or a dig?"

"Oh. Apologies. I wasn't aware you sought a position in that field."

She stares at me for a moment. "To answer your question, there're a handful of local kids through the different year groups. The smart ones."

"Right. Kai was too stupid. Understood."

"Violet! Don't say that to his face."

"I already have in a roundabout way." Holly sighs at me. "But his lack of intelligence could be helpful if I want to read his mind." Locating my phone, I shove it into my sweater pocket.

"Don't mind read either. You know it's illegal."

Oh, that's nothing compared to the illegal things I'm planning.

"He won't notice."

She narrows her eyes. "I hope you and Rowan aren't plotting something that could cause trouble."

"Good grief, no. I'd prefer a low profile tonight."

"Right." Her disbelief couldn't be clearer now I'm learning her ways. "And why aren't you going with Rowan? Are you avoiding him again?"

Ah. Rowan. Behaving as if that time in the rain never happened. Reverse psychology, perhaps? "That's impossible, since we share classes. I'm meeting him there."

"I've told you before, be careful around Rowan."

"Your concern is unwarranted. I have him in hand." I pause. "What are you giggling at?" Holly sucks her lips together and shakes her head. "What is suddenly amusing?"

"That's what Rowan's waiting for." Holly continues to snicker as she opens the door.

I frown at the back of her head. Personal jokes. More human code I've yet to decipher.

THE ONLY PARTIES I'VE HAD THE MISFORTUNE OF ATTENDING were rare occasions at home where Dorian and Eloise would invite close friends.

So never big parties.

Occasionally, these guests brought offspring, and I'd amuse myself in ways that didn't amuse the child. That's where I began to hear my new 'name' Violet.

I also avoided all invites to parties at the human school—the *one* invite since I only attended for a couple of months and my popularity level never left bottom floor.

Despite automatically declining a party invitation, tonight became unavoidable. Not only will this aid in our investigations into the killings, but I also get an opportunity to meet more of the town's humans. I never interacted with human kids at the fire or the memorial; I'm curious to see their reaction to me and their true thoughts on the murders.

Finding any evidence of Petrescu influence inside the Sawyers' home would also help immensely.

Kai's house befits the position of a man on the town council who took over and expanded a profitable family business. Who knew canned soup could raise such a fortune? The two story home resembles a rectangular, gray box with an unnecessary amount of glass, and looks out of place with every other home I've seen in the area. My stone-bricked home takes up a small piece of the Scottish estate and blends in; this house is built to dominate the land the upper windows look over.

I can't see much of the estate through the dark, as the Sawyer's factory is also located too far to see. After all, why would they want to spoil their view with an industrial building?

Holly walks us around the rear of the home. Kids spill out across a large paved terrace that leads to the rectangular pool containing nonsensical, semi-naked people. Half-empty cans and bottles are strewn across a long marble-topped table that's surrounded by chairs. Citrus trees add more to the Mediterranean aesthetic, and the square planters have edges wide enough to sit on.

The majority of the noise comes from inside the house through open doors that span the whole length of the room, although those splashing and screeching in the pool definitely add decibels.

I'm on the verge of running before my head explodes from the unpleasant amount of noise and exuberant energy.

"I think we should remain outside," I tell Holly. "Where I can breathe, while I wait for Rowan."

Holly rubs her pink-painted lips together. "I'll head inside and fetch us drinks. Are you sure you're okay on your own?"

"In current circumstances, alone is impossible."

With a wry smile, Holly ducks through a group who're crowding the way into the house. Briefly regarding those around, pleased I know none of them and won't be forced to speak yet, I move to my semi-hidden area.

Where's Rowan?

There're academy kids here, but so far I don't recognize any of Wesley's closer friends. Alibi or not, Kai isn't off my suspect list yet—for Rory's murder at least, although two separate killers makes little sense. But whatever hellish evening I'm subjecting myself to, I've plenty to absorb from the evening's social networking. These kids' love of alcohol should aid with my questioning.

Two guys climb out of the pool, wet skin gleaming beneath the star-like party-lights strung around the perimeter. I stare and not because they're semi-naked but because they're witches I've seen around the academy. The one with his long, black curls tied from his face once interrogated me about Holly's likes and dislikes, for reasons I can't fathom.

Witches. How curious. Holly mentioned academy kids would attend, but I didn't expect such a social mix—the supes and humans appeared separate at the fire yet mingle here.

Holly takes her time and I blow air into my cheeks before sitting on the wooden bench connecting two lemon tree-filled planters. Rowan agreed to meet me outside and I'm irritated he isn't here. A rebuff for me refusing to attend together?

Rowan may not be here, but somebody else is.

Chapter Seventeen

VIOLET

I smell Grayson before I see him, body jolting to alert as his scent filters through the cloud of cologne and chlorine in the air. Grayson doesn't see me since a couple of humans stand in front of where I sit, but his head turns in my direction the moment I spy him through the gap.

No leather jacket tonight—plain jeans, and Converse sneakers, a black T-shirt fitted to his lithe frame. I'm always suspicious when vamps wear black—blood stains are less likely to show. The lights strung across the terrace roof cast a rainbow of colors across his paler skin, but none can compete with his eyes.

Eyes that catch mine.

As Grayson approaches, the couple in front of me sidestep, an automatic response by humans, even when not realizing they're close to a vampire. He blocks my view of others around him as he looks down.

"I hear you've been looking for me, Violet."

His blood. I swallow the saliva filling my mouth at the scent of him. "Who told you?"

"Ah!" He grins. "Nobody. But now I know you have. Strange, since you've avoided me for days."

"You've avoided me too," I bat back.

As Grayson sits on the bench, I spring to my feet before his scent overwhelms me. When he stood close and looked down, my blood desire rose uncomfortably, but he remained still, which helped. This does not.

"Wow. Do I smell that bad?"

You have no idea. "I have something I want to talk to you about."

"Grayson!" Holly reappears at my side and thrusts a red cup into my hand. "I didn't know you're invited."

Each moment he stares at me, the more breath he seems to suck away, and I curse Holly's awesome timing.

Grayson runs his tongue along his bottom lip, eyes shining. "I'm a friend of Kai's."

"You are?" I grip the cold cup.

"Yeah. My reputation for dealing with Wes's gang on campus adds to my popularity."

"So Kai *didn't* like Wes?" I ask.

"Nah. Doesn't like anyone who's friends with Viggo. Wes was."

A girl with sleek brown hair stumbles closer and calls out 'hello' to him. Grayson responds with a nod, and she changes course towards a group of girls drinking from bottles, sitting at the edge of the pool.

"And popularity with girls?" I ask, nodding towards her.

He flicks his tongue against his teeth. "Human girls still have a thing for vamps my age. I can thank human books and movies for that. Right, Holly?"

"Not me," she retorts.

"Oh? You're here to find a willing participant, Grayson?" I arch a brow.

"No." He's vehement enough that I shrink back. "If you don't want tarring as a Blackwood, don't tar a Petrescu."

"Good grief. Calm down." Stone-cold silence follows before Grayson walks away. Should I follow?

"I'm not sure I like Grayson," says Holly solemnly, and sips from her cup.

"My opinion of him is confused too." I sniff the cup. "What is this?"

"Beer."

Grimacing, I tip the contents into a planter and Holly tuts at me. "Come into the house."

And find Rowan?

Taking a calming breath, I step through the doors into a high-ceilinged room, and I'm overwhelmed by the music and voices, the sheer volume of people inside here cloying my senses. I'm sure that Kai's parents wouldn't want their white leather sofas covered in whatever the curly-haired girl just spilled from her cup as she tripped, nor trampled by the lanky guy using the sofa and glass-topped table as a route across the room.

No Rowan, but Holly pauses to chat to Isabella close to a door that leads into the kitchen. She stands beneath a family studio portrait featuring all three Sawyers and a small fluffy white dog. I hope for the dog's sake that it isn't around tonight.

Isabella looks at me through unfocused eyes. "Smile. You're pretty when you do. Maybe we can hook you up with a cute guy."

I scowl harder. "Look at who you're speaking to and reconsider that statement."

"True. The sour face won't help," replies Isabella.

"Grayson already hit on her," says Holly, and glances around the over-filled room.

"Grayson never hit me. He wouldn't be standing if he did."

Holly gives a wry smile. "Hit *on.*"

"Grayson's still trying then?" Isabella asks.

"Trying to what? Assault me?"

"To get you into his bed and his teeth in your neck," says Isabella and drains her drink. *Good grief.* "He's likely pissed at your resistance to his skills."

"And he has many conquests?"

Isabella chuckles at my choice of words. "He has a reputation, but a couple of mistakes mean most on campus keep away."

Our conversation takes place amidst a greater cacophony than outside where at least the thumping music drifted into the night. I vow this first will also be my last party.

"Gray doesn't touch girls on campus anymore. Probably goes elsewhere for his fixes," says Isabella. "Most developing hemia do okay with animal blood. Grayson? The other vamps say no."

I half-laugh at my 'misunderstood loner' comment from the first time we met.

"Gray probably thinks he's safe with you because you're stronger and won't end up in the infirmary when he takes too much." Isabella's burbling continues, and I grit my teeth. Avoiding campus society has left me on the edge of a lot of knowledge I need. As has my rudeness and disdain, which again I'm forced to swallow in order to get answers. "Or hospital. One girl needed a transfusion—almost died."

"What?" I snap my attention back to Isabella. "Didn't they expel him?"

"Nope. Gave him a second chance—risky," says Isabella.

This isn't a common situation, but I'm lost for words. My attraction to Grayson's blood is a desire for someone with a darker side than most vampires? "But he's stopped attacking people?"

"Like I said, nobody goes near. The other vamps say Gray heads off campus three nights a week. I guess he has other willing participants." She huffs. "What are we talking about him for? We'll find another guy for you."

"She's meeting Rowan," says Holly.

Isabella pulls a face. "That figures."

"I don't understand your phrase. Have you seen Rowan?"

"No. Why would I look for the weird witch? He'd probably hex me," replies Isabella.

"Unlikely. Rowan wouldn't waste magic on something as insignificant as you."

"O-*kay*." Holly pulls at my sleeve. "This way, Violet."

Annoyed at Rowan's continuous absence, I follow Holly to the kitchen and fill my cup with water from the faucet while she pours herself another beer.

"Considering your current mental state regarding your failed relationship with Ollie, I advise against consuming too much alcohol," I inform Holly, half-inclined to take the cup from her hand. The last thing I need is Holly wandering off and dying.

"Yes, Mother," she says.

"Why are you calling me your mother?"

She smiles. "I'm alright now—I'm moving on. There're other cute guys."

Oh, the fickleness of humans and their constant need for validation. "You don't need a guy in your life, Holly."

She drinks her beer. "Nothing serious. Some fun."

Aware that Holly's gazing through the open kitchen door to the lounge area, I follow her line of vision. The witch from the pool—now wearing a T-shirt and also smiling in a way that puts a weird look on Holly's face.

"You already look drunk. Your eyes are glazed and cheeks pink," I tell her. "How? You've had one drink."

"I think Chase might be interested in me," she whispers. "He's spoken to me a couple of times recently."

"What kind of name is Chase?" I glance back at where

the witch's focus remains on Holly. "Or is this a moniker because he commonly pursues girls?"

Holly waves a hand at me. "Shush."

"Excuse me?"

The incomparable Chase appears in front of us, the two locked together with smiles. "Hey, Holly."

Now they're both looking at me. Silently. Should something in Holly's expression communicate a thought?

"Maybe look for Rowan?" she asks, as she inclines a head to Chase, who's now looking in the fridge.

Oh.

Hmm.

"Don't go out of sight," I inform her. "There's a killer on the loose."

"I doubt the killer attended the party," says Chase as he turns back.

"Why? There's a choice selection of victims." Holly's eyes widen at my reply. "We should hope I don't argue with anybody, since that's the common denominator amongst past victims."

"Violet!" says Holly.

"Common what?" asks Chase.

Most humans really do have a limited vocabulary. "People I argue with die."

"Violet!" repeats Holly, louder, as Chase stares at me, open-mouthed. "Find Rowan."

"Good idea. I'll be back soon. Don't leave," I say firmly and walk away.

Chapter Eighteen

VIOLET

I DON'T BELIEVE THE NIGHT WILL END WITH MURDER, BUT hopefully drunk teens stay out of the woods. The killer wouldn't act publicly, but still, I don't rate these humans' natural survival instincts.

I can't pass from the kitchen without brushing against someone, and I pause long enough that the human obstacles detect the 'off' energy close to them. One guy looks at me; I smile, thin-lipped, and he shuffles out of the way.

Where's Rowan? Speaking to Kai? I can't see either amongst the seething mass of human frivolity. A glass shelved, pale wood dresser dominates the room, and I pause, looking at each object, fingers itching to touch. There're a lot of white porcelain figurines with detailed painted faces, including a dog that resembles the one in the portrait. Nothing out of the ordinary.

There're photos too, Kai's father in a suit, accepting shiny silver awards, smiling, and shaking hands with others. Some of those awards are arranged on the shelves—accolades for superior soup recipes? Blowing air into my cheeks, I peruse the other photographs. A town council group—I recognize the mayor. Kai in full football gear with an award of his own beside it. Why am I not surprised he's an accomplished sportsman?

Rowan only found one picture of the Petrescus and the Sawyers online, but here there're several. The hemia features are easy to spot and both share Grayson's midnight brown hair and emerald eyes. Am I looking at one of the killers? Rowan checked whether the couple are Grayson's parents and I was excessively relieved to discover they're not.

"Not too bothered about me being an unintelligent human who buys his popularity anymore?"

I take a deep breath and turn. We'd agreed Rowan would speak to Kai while I snooped. This is not good. Will Kai escort me from the premises before I manage to seize his mind and stop him? He swigs from his bottle and looks at me with unfocused eyes.

"I'm rude to everybody. I have an... issue," I reply.

"Mental?" He swigs again.

I carefully reach out to Kai's mind. "Some would suggest that."

"Yeah. Got a cousin who's on the spectrum. He's like you. Needs to watch his mouth." Kai raises a brow.

I am thoroughly confused. "Spectrum of what?"

He shrugs. Evidently alcohol or me being 'mental' dampens Kai's hostility. I fight to hide my disdain—do humans always judge and label each other in such inappropriate and negative ways? Well, I can use *mental* magic on him.

"I'll take that," says Kai as he removes the silver frame from my hand before peering at it. "First time I saw that, the image confused me. Thought vampires didn't appear in photos or mirrors."

"I'm half-vampire and I rarely do. I avoid both." I take

the frame back, wanting to confirm I'm looking at the right couple, and then slip into his mind. Oddly, this is harder than I thought, as if there's a slight barrier. The alcohol? "Are these people family friends or business acquaintances?"

Kai rubs his head a moment and frowns. "Both. The guy's our attorney. Known him since I was a kid." He again takes the frame. Does he know I'm a thief too? "One reason I'm not bothered by vamps."

Aha. *Don't worry about the questions I'm asking, Kai.* He swats around his head as if a fly buzzed in his ear.

"'Do you know if he's related to Grayson?" I ask. "He's Petrescu too."

"Huh? Really? I don't know Gray well enough to know his surname."

"You haven't seen them together?"

"Nah. But Josef rarely comes to town. He's a city attorney. Good one. Expensive one." He chews on his lip and lowers his voice. "Helped me against a shifter assault charge."

Oh? "A business attorney did?" He nods. "And you've met him?"

"Yeah. Weird guy. Intense. Him and Dad are close though."

Hmm. "Which is why you're okay with supes?"

"Uh huh. Though Dad's selective about who he lets into the house—he'd probably lose his shit if he knew I'd invited a load of kids from the academy." Kai continues to burble, easily prompted by alcohol, and so I barely require magic at all. "Dad isn't a witch fan."

More than the items on the shelf distract me as I stare at Kai's chest. Oddly, I don't have the same response to his as I did to Grayson's, but I suppose he was semi-naked. Plus, I've no interest in Kai's blood.

No. A *necklace* catches my eye, or rather the small pendant. Silver and circular with a hole in the center and a matching chain threaded through. Black letters are etched on the pendant.

And it's magic.

"I like your necklace, where is it from?" I ask.

He folds his fingers around the pendant. "Huh? I've had this for years. Dad wears one too."

Does he now? "And you like to emulate your father." Blank look. "Be like him."

"Well, I'd like his money." Kai chuckles.

"How mercenary." He scowls at me. "And do you remove the pendant often, or are you told to wear it at all times?"

"Do you think it's magic?" he says with a laugh.

"Yes."

"It's just a necklace."

"How do you know?"

Kai's mouth twists with scorn. "What do you think my *magic necklace* is?"

"Hey, Kai!" An inebriated teen knocks into him, pulling Kai from my influence as he wraps an arm around his shoulder. "Look."

The guy with a crew cut to match Kai's holds up his phone for Kai to watch the screen and, although I see little, I can hear a lot of shouting. "What the fuck? When was this?" snaps Kai.

"Earlier. Assholes waited outside school and attacked TJ and Dan."

"Who did? Show me."

The guy fixes drunken eyes on me. "You're that weird kid who fought the shifters."

"The one and only. What's on your phone?"

He hiccups and turns the screen to me. Unsurprisingly, the clip depicts Viggo and his friends besting kids who must be TJ and Dan.

"Were the shifters arrested?" I ask.

"Yeah. But all that happens is authorities then hand the

assholes over to their own for 'punishment', which doesn't change anything," says Kai.

"And you theorize that the shifters killed Rory, Kai?" I say and watch for a reaction.

He shrugs. "Don't care. At least they can't touch me."

"Oh?" I ask sharply and eye his pendant. "What makes you special?"

"My father would kick the whole pack of animals off his land. He allows them to live on the part he doesn't use, so all this bullshit about our family stealing from them isn't true."

"Land he bought and owns?"

"Yeah."

"That once belonged to shifters?"

"Yeah."

"And you can't see why him owning and giving 'permission' is a problem?" I shake my head. "How very human and stupid."

"Watch your mouth," he says sharply, then looks back to his friend. "Are the guys okay?"

"Smashed faces and TJ has a broken arm. The bastard animals are out of control," he says, lip curling. "You gotta do something, Kai."

"I advise against that," I interrupt. "Especially if you believe they're instrumental in Rory's and possibly Wesley's deaths."

"Like I said, they can't touch me." He drains his drink. "Right. They crashed Wes's memorial and funeral, we'll 'attend' Rory's wake tomorrow."

I straighten, once again stunned by human unintelligence. "Excuse me?"

"Like I said, using Dad's land for their 'sacred rites' or whatever." I don't need to understand his tone to set alarm bells ringing. "Hey, you and Rowan could join us. Help with our vermin problem."

And these people all stood around a fire together, supposedly in harmony?

"Ah, Rowan!" calls Kai and waves behind me.

Rowan stands in a doorway across the room, and I sense the magical brightness around him. As Rowan strides over, I mouth, 'where have you been?' and he inclines his head towards the doorway.

Well, *obviously*.

"Dale wasn't at the memorial, tell him what you did, mate." Kai claps Rowan on the back and Rowan's whole body tenses. "Reckon you could do that to shifters again?"

"Why?" he asks.

"Just chatting to your girlfriend about joining us for a shifter visit tomorrow."

"Um. I prefer to keep away from shifters. We both do," he replies and does not correct Kai on the 'girlfriend' part.

Rowan's eyes slide to mine as Kai proceeds to tell him about his plans. I nod at Kai and tap my neck. He frowns, so I shake my necklace at him, and the witch finally looks at Kai's neck.

"I need to steal Violet for a moment," Rowan says to Kai. "Then I'll be back."

Rowan's hand goes to my lower back, and he guides me to the edge of the room. I resist pushing his hand away since that would look weird to everybody around us but move away as soon as we reach the wall.

"Steal me?" I ask in disbelief.

"I'm surprised Kai's talking to you after you insulted him. Are you using magic?" he asks. I suck my lips together and he sighs. "*Subtly*, I hope."

"You're the one who's supposed to speak to him! My conversing with Kai was accidental and because you weren't there." I scowl. "Do you at least know what that pendant is?"

"No. Do you?"

"Protection, maybe?" I crane my neck, annoyed at having

to half-shout above the mind-numbing music. "Have you looked around the house? Is that where you were?"

"Was late. Sorry."

"Great," I mutter. "Well, guess who else is here?" He shrugs. "The elusive Grayson Petrescu. Coincidence?"

Rowan darts a look around. "Where? Did you ask him about Sawyer's Petrescu attorney?"

"Never had the chance, but I will by the end of the night —if Grayson hasn't left. You talk to Kai and get details about his foolish plans. We need to go to the shifter's wake."

"No, we bloody don't," retorts Rowan. "You need to be somewhere that a large number of people see you all day, in case something happens to anybody else."

I give him a long look. "I'll search upstairs first."

"Violet are you listening to me?" he asks sternly.

"You talk to Kai." I turn away from him. I don't have time for a Rowan clash.

"Fine. Careful in case some rooms are occupied," he says, and I look back.

"Aren't his parents away?"

"Oh, Violet..."

"'Oh, Violet' what?"

Rowan inclines his head to where a couple are kissing, propped against a wall.

I've seen enough of Holly's shows to know exactly what he means. "Teenagers are disgusting."

Taking a deep breath, I prepare to plow through the humans.

Chapter Nineteen

VIOLET

THE HOUSE SMELLS DIFFERENT UPSTAIRS, A FRESH CLEAN SCENT from the plush carpet beneath my booted feet and a strong smell of cleaning products—pine and a horrific fake rose.

Couples crowd the stairs and hallway, helpfully paying little attention to my presence. I'm instantly aware which room is the bathroom as that door seems the most popular to loiter by, and I'm surprised by how many others are open. I'd hoped one might be a study, but that's too much to wish for. Besides, I've downstairs rooms to check too.

Several bedrooms later, I enter the last, again frustrated that the room isn't Sawyer's study. Definitely the master—the thick-carpeted room could fit two of the other bedrooms inside and the open plan wardrobe could house a small family. I turn my head to the ensuite where I spy plush pink towels that match the carpets draped over the edge of a jacuzzi.

Kai's parents' room?

I'm about to turn away when I sense something. Magic. But where?

If Kai's father doesn't like witches entering his home, is he aware there's something magical in his bedroom? I close my eyes and focus, but the energy is faint. Coming from close to the cushion covered bed?

"Whatcha doing in here?" asks a male voice from behind.

"She's waiting for someone," says a second.

Pissed at the interruption, I snap my eyes open and turn. Two bulky human guys with buzz cuts, one with a beer bottle in his hand and the other beside him, arms crossed, stand in the doorway.

Wesley's friends.

I sigh inwardly. I've avoided the majority of students connected to Wesley since his murder and hoped to maintain that situation. The pair need to leave if I'm to continue my search because I swear there's something close by. Mind control the idiots away from me?

As I reach out with my magic, one steps closer in an attempt to intimidate me with his muscular frame, and I throw a spell at him. The energy bounces back. *What?*

I'm aware of the second guy moving to stand beside me and I hold the first one's gaze. Are they completely stupid?

"You killed Wes," says the guy facing me.

"I'd advise you to move," I say evenly. Why can't I touch this one's mind? The barrier my magic hit remind hard and black.

"Why? You gonna hurt me?" Beer on his breath turns my stomach as he's in my face. "Go on. We saw what you can do when you attacked the shifters. That what you did to Wes?"

The magic sparks in my veins, automatically pulled to the surface by a threat, however pathetic. The guy behind me stands close enough to smell his cheap cologne.

Far too close.

"Yeah. Show us how you deal with people you don't like,

Blackwood." The breath of the guy behind ruffles my hair and fires up that magic further, and I mentally shove him backwards. Hard. The guy thuds as he hits the wall, but a moment later he's back behind me. "You can do better than that."

No. Every Blackwood instinct screams at me to deal with these assholes as I did the shifters, to not stop until they're terrified or injured, but I take calming breaths.

They want me to attack them. That's why the idiots are here.

I spot a third guy in the doorway, holding up a phone to film our encounter, confirming my theory this is planned and deliberate. My eyes dart to the doors leading onto a balcony. Are they unlocked? I could vacate the room that way.

And how do I stop myself from reacting? These humans are easy opponents, and I could physically or magically hit them into next week.

At this moment, I almost hate my father for sending me away and putting me in a position like this. His powerful hybrid daughter reduced to a weakling because she's strong. Didn't he consider I'd find myself in a situation where using my powers would be as dangerous to me as *not* using them?

The asshole facing me wears a partially unbuttoned black shirt and I double take. A chain with a coin-like silver pendant attached. I'm unable to see the words but, like Kai's, the thing exudes magic.

Magic that creates a barrier against me around his mind. Why didn't Kai's?

"Who gave you that necklace?" I ask sharply. The guy behind moves closer and I hiss as my vampire stirs. "A witch?"

"Was Wes's," he snarls. "I'm wearing it to remember him. He was my best mate."

"You took the necklace from his body?" I ask.

His lip curls. "What type of sicko do you think I am? You accusing me?"

"Then where did you get Wesley's necklace?" I ask, darting another look around for a safe exit. Did he rifle through police evidence too?

"His room."

I'm not calming as they continue to close in on me, and if I have to endure this to get information, I need my Blackwood nature under control.

But if they touch me.

Kai and Wesley both own protection talismans? "Who gave *Wesley* that?"

"Dunno." He leans forward, his disgusting face in mine. "You can't hurt me little Blackwood because everyone will see that clip when we upload it. What are you going to do to Raul if he touches you? Kill him too?"

Calm. Calm. Calm.

As a hand reaches from behind and seizes me around the neck, the magic careens through and to the surface. "Get your hand off me!" I yell.

Raul shrieks as if he's burned himself and drops his hold, and darkness pushes through, obliterating my control. I spin around to face Raul, stepping forward and smacking him in the chest. My supernatural strength slams him into the wall again, and he stumbles, knocking a tasseled lamp from the nightstand.

"Don't touch me." I advance on him, and he presses himself back harder, terror masking his face as mine takes on vampire features—the *little Blackwood* now black-eyed, lips drawn back to expose the sharper teeth that can and will rip into him if he tries anything else.

And I *want* to.

"What the fuck, man?" Raul croaks out to the protected guy. "Logan. Stop her."

"She needs to hurt one of us. Looks like you drew the short straw." Logan chuckles, but I barely register the words as my vision and hearing sharpen. I'm not attracted to Raul's blood and don't want a taste, but I'll happily spill it.

"I hardly touched you!" he says to me wildly.

Closing my eyes, I tip my head and take a long breath, heart pumping with shadow-filled anger. No, he didn't, but I caught a glimpse of his intentions, and he wasn't stopping at my neck. They were prepared to push me until I got to this point.

With a snarl, I lunge at him, then cry out as somebody grabs my hair and yanks me backwards. I scream and suck in deep breaths, preparing magic against *this* attacker instead, as a commotion breaks out behind me.

"Stay still," grits out a voice. "Stop what you're doing. I'll deal with this."

Grayson. My eyes water as I pant out my fury, snarling at him to let me go, now unable to see what's happening.

He drops his grip, and my scalp tingles as I pull my head forward and turn. One guy lies on the floor and Grayson's hand is now around Logan's neck, lifting him from the floor as he did Wesley the night in the cloisters.

Chapter Twenty

VIOLET

Grayson glances at those he knocked to the carpet, still grasping the choking guy.

"How many fucking times? Leave supes alone," he snarls.

"Take his pendant off," I growl.

Grayson reaches out and tears at the chain until it breaks. "I should snap your neck, asshole."

"*You* helped her kill Wes?" Logan chokes out a laugh. "Figures, since you threatened Wes enough times."

"Believe me, if I killed any of you, nobody would find the bodies, Logan." Grayson yanks him forward by the neck. "There wouldn't be enough left."

Clawing back more control before my dark side is tempted to join in, I dart a look between Grayson and the doorway. How many people can hear this? There're a few more kids now crowded in the space, and more than one phone pointed in our direction.

Again, the desire for self-protection pushes at me, suggesting I could deal with them all. *That's what they want, and*

I've already done too much. I drop onto the edge of the bed and take slow breaths. "Grayson. Put him down."

The other dumb human who attacked already shoved through the gathering crowd and out of the room—but three others now hold their phones in our direction.

I sense Rowan before he reaches the room and pauses, open-mouthed, and I shake my head at him as he looks around, assessing the scene. "No magic. Don't make this worse. Please. Stop the filming. That'll help."

Face grim, Rowan swipes at the nearest phone and knocks it from a hand. I rise again and step forward, pulling myself straight and fixing a malevolent look on those outside the room. I don't need to go further before the kids falter, phones looser in their hands.

Rowan fixates on the phones, one by one, until they glow and spark in their hands. Shrieking as the items become electrified, kids drop each one to the floor. I snarl and step further forward, while Rowan lifts a foot and stomps on a phone before anybody can respond up. Not that any hang around the hallway anymore.

"Where's Kai?" yells a guy.

Beside me, Grayson doesn't let Logan go, and he's choking half to death.

"Grayson, stop!" I shout at him as Rowan violently stamps the phones on the carpet. "We need to stop. This is what they want."

"I don't care." Grayson slams the guy against the wall. "I've seen into their minds. What they want to do to supes— not only you."

"Let go!" I shout at him, that much vampire in my veins that I easily pull him away from Logan. Grayson flies backwards at the force and smashes into the glass door, the impact managing to break and shatter the safety glass.

Grayson swears and pushes himself up from where he

lands on his back, on the balcony, and I falter as something else takes over.

No. *No.* Blood. My entire being focuses on Grayson's *blood* and I force myself to step backwards.

"Violet?" I whip my head around to where Holly stands pale faced beside Rowan, who continues to vent his fury at the phones.

"Rowan. Take Holly back to the academy," I croak out.

"You're bleeding. Omigod, what happened here?" she cries.

I wipe the wet beneath my nose and stare in horror, then swipe at my eyes too and look at fingers covered in blood.

"Rowan. Look after Holly," I urge him when Holly's words snap him out of his frenzy. "Get her out." He jerks his head around, faint shadows forming around him as he sees Logan on the carpet. "Rowan! Get Holly out of here before she passes out or something happens to her!"

Before he unleashes too.

"But you——" he begins.

"I'm alright. I've hurt Grayson and need to help him."

I wipe a hand across my mouth. Why am I lying? The only thing I want right now is his blood, so intensely that it's preventing me walking through the door with my friends.

"Kai!" Another yell, this time from outside, below the balcony.

Mouthing an apology, I slam the door closed and spin around towards the broken glass doors. Grayson presses his back to the balcony rail outside, fingers on his wounds as he heals the scratches.

"How bad?" I ask.

"How bad do I want your blood or how bad do I hurt?" he rasps out.

"Don't," I say and force myself to stay still.

"I knew you felt the same." He shakes his head and moves his hand to push against another scratch. The sharp scent from his blood assaults me even though he's stemmed most of the bleeding. "How long did it take for you to notice too?"

"Notice what?" I moisten my lips and swallow down the rising desire.

"How attracted to my blood you are." Grayson thankfully remains still, but his eyes are flicking between my face and his bloodied hands.

"I'm not."

"Don't you think I felt a change in you that night, Violet?" he whispers. "Your response to tasting my blood."

"Don't be ridiculous." If I edge back now, I'll support his theory, so hold my ground.

"Remember the night at the graveyard when I said I could smell you? I've never picked up on another's blood scent like that, ever." He slants his head. "I'd decided this was one-sided from my attraction to you, until you bit me. Violet, the way you looked at me as I held you against that tree."

"You're ridiculous," I repeat. "I did not appreciate your physical restraint. My look was a warning I'd attack you."

The laugh bursting from him bounces around us. "Have you tasted anybody's blood before?"

"No. That wasn't a lie."

"You won't constrain yourself forever."

"I will."

"Violet, you're half-vampire. Hemia vampires grow into their blood desires. If nothing else, instinct will get you."

"You should go," I warn.

"You're struggling. So am I."

"Grayson. Walk away." I hold a hand over my mouth and nose as he ignores me and moves closer. Grayson healed most of his cuts, but blood streaks his bare arms, and a scratch runs along his cheek. He's insane. "Okay, I admit it. You're right. Back up," I say, voice muffled.

He wipes beneath my eye, and my thudding heart stutters at his touch. For a moment, Grayson stares at my blood on his fingertip before wiping onto his jeans. I can't stop shaking as I battle the vampire Violet who's still clawing her way out—the one who wanted to kill tonight. Now Grayson's blood screams out to her, and I desperately grasp at anything left in my mind that can stop me before I fall completely into a place I have no control.

"Violet. Listen."

Grayson takes a fatal step closer, the move shoving me over the edge and into that dark place. Blinded, I seize hold of his shirt and drag him towards me, the taste of Grayson's blood already imagined on my tongue.

"Fuck!" He staggers backwards and manages to get hold of me.

My arms are trapped between us, bodies almost flush, and I'm seconds away from biting and taking his blood into my mouth.

Grayson stills for a moment, and I meet his eyes, emerald obliterated by black. He grabs my wrists, digging nails into them until I yelp and release him. In a heartbeat, I'm on the floor, slamming into the nightstand and knocking it over as he shoves me away. The globe shatters as the nightstand lands sideways on top of the lamp. Grayson strides over and looks down at me and as I leap back to my feet, he pushes me against a wall, my wrists in his hand, panting down at me.

I'd surpass him magically, but this full-blooded vampire is physically stronger than my vamp half.

"Do you understand the amount of self-control this is taking, Violet?" he says, voice hoarse, face shifted into hemia features. "How much I want to give you what you want—and take what you'd offer?"

I moisten my lips and swallow down the desperation.

"But I need you to understand that I'm powerful. Petrescus didn't once hold high positions for their persuasive skills. Your father knows we're his biggest threat." He takes a shuddery breath. "I'm the closest to anything that can match you, Violet. You won't weaken or hurt me."

"I don't want to," I rasp out. "Your blood."

I'm pissed at how easily both of my wrists fit in one of his hands and he moistens a thumb to wipe drying blood from beneath my nose, a finger brushing my lips. "You don't want me," he whispers. "You're not *choosing* this reaction, and that's why I'm walking away."

I look back, wide-eyed. "No, but—"

"Until you know who you are and what you want, Violet, I'm not touching you."

"You appear to be doing so right now."

"And Violet Blackwood hates touch. Therefore, you are not her right now." His fingers grasp my wrists harder. "I'm going to walk away. Don't follow me. Go downstairs and deal with the crap we've created."

"*You* created," I retort, as my senses react to his words.

He half-smiles. "Another reason I should leave."

Grayson's emerald irises begin to reappear, the black fading, but his breathing remains harsh. He stares at my mouth then looks back to me as Rowan did that day, then presses his thumb to his mouth and then places it on my lips, the pad rough to the touch. My breath hitches as the blood lust ebbs. He's right. This isn't me.

So why when I look at a calmer Grayson is my heart still racing?

I blink as he bolts away from me towards the balcony and springs over the edge. I'm lost in a haze of confusion and physical want—I can't differentiate if that's blood or something more, barely listening to the continuing shouts and banging downstairs.

Finally bringing my breathing back to normal, I look at the damage in the room and grimace. I can put everything back into place, but how will Kai explain this? Academy kids destroyed his parents' property. The fall out will be horrendous.

The nightstand weighs little and is intact, so I pull it from the floor.

Then pause. A black rune on the carpet in the place the nightstand should be. I drop to my knees and look more closely, tracing the shape with my fingers. Protection rune.

Unsure how long I have, I leap to my feet and move to shove away the nightstand on the other side of the bed.

The same rune.

Dragging my hands through my hair, I step back and look from side to side at the identical marks.

What do the Sawyers need protecting from?

Carefully, I slide the nightstand back into place, finally focused away from Grayson and his blood. Before I can reach the balcony, the bedroom door flies open again.

Kai.

I'm still not great at reading body language, but everything about him yells fury.

"What the fuck did you do, Violet?" he shouts. "You've trashed my parents' bedroom and attacked people!"

I swallow. "Kai. This wasn't me."

"Uh. Wrong. Your witch might've broken the phones, but there're a lot of witnesses," he continues to shout.

"Kai. Calm down."

"Calm down? My parents didn't know about this party and now look!" He drags both hands down his face. "There's a guy down there half-choked and others covered in bruises. A whole fucking fight broke out. The police are on the way."

"Please," I whisper. "Don't fight with me."

He sneers. "Not so superior and cocky now, huh? Scared what I'll do? What people will say?"

"Don't fight with me," I repeat.

"Why? Will you attack me too?"

"Don't say that. Kai."

What do I do? Since arriving at Thornwood, everybody I clash badly with dies. I can't tell Kai to walk away because someone might attack him—or worse. And if I do say the words, and he's hurt, everybody watching can testify that I threatened Kai.

The killer might be one of those crowded in the doorway watching us, or downstairs amid the chaos, ready to take advantage of the situation.

Did our actions tonight sign another death warrant?

Chapter Twenty-One

VIOLET

Rowan sits in my desk chair and Holly snuggles beneath one of her fluffy blankets, each competing for who has the palest face. The blanket falls away as Holly stands, dressed in the same outfit as earlier, but her curls wilder.

"Omigod, you're back. I worried they arrested you." She darts over to hug me, and I take an automatic step back.

"I left before the police arrived," I say, one eye on Rowan who's slumped back, legs crossed, silently scrutinizing me.

I've no idea what chaos broke out downstairs in Kai's house, and I didn't hang around to find out. My only course of action became an evasive move over the balcony before my exchange of words with Kai became a full blown argument.

"I'm happy you left before the local riot began," I say. No response from Rowan. "I should wash my face."

Stepping into the bathroom, I close the door and rest my hands on the sink, peering at myself. Blood streaks down my face like dried tears and there're smudges around my mouth too. Trembling, I touch my lips.

What's happening to me?

Bleeding when overcome by the hybrid magic is common, but the speed I switched into attack mode and then wanted to tear into Grayson is not me. I dip my head forward and my long hair touches the porcelain. What now? A criminal damage charge? Assault conviction from the Thornwood students?

That pales against my fear Kai could die—or one of the Darwin house kids who attacked me. I don't want another murder charge, and death won't be a good outcome for the victim.

The door creaks open and Holly sidles through, throwing a quick glance back at Rowan. "I'm glad you're here. Rowan scares me."

"What did he do?" I ask sharply.

"Nothing. He brought me from the party to our room, but then refused to leave. There's something off about him." She chews on her lip. "He's always been odd, but now Rowan seems completely unstable."

"That's my influence." I grab a washcloth from beneath the sink and dampen it.

Holly watches me through the mirror as I wipe away my blood before she sits on the edge of the bath. "How?"

For a few moments, I don't answer, focusing on cleaning my face. "Two witches. One who loses control when the other is under threat and then won't calm down?"

The answer clicks into place, and her mouth slackens. "You're bonded? Omigod!"

"Yes," I mutter. "And you can see the effect this has on me. I'm not in control of myself anymore, and neither is Rowan."

"Oh." Surprisingly, she doesn't shuffle away. "I did notice you're engaging with me more."

"And engaging with parts of myself I shouldn't." I screw up the wash cloth and throw it into the linen basket. "And

Rowan's more powerful magically with me, which is dangerous. I'm glad Grayson got to me before Rowan tonight."

"*I'm* not. Grayson threatened to kill Logan," she says in a hushed tone.

"Only a threat. But I believe Rowan *would* have killed Logan." I stare at my clean skin, devoid of blood and make-up. I've no doubt. Rowan turned magically psychotic when the shifters threatened me—these guys physically assaulted his bonded witch.

"This is too much for me, Violet. I'm tired and want to go to bed." Holly's shoulders drop. "The party became a riot —I bet the place is trashed. We got away before anyone realized what happened upstairs, but there're a lot of witnesses. What if I'm accused of something because you were with *me*?"

"I'll inform authorities that I mind controlled you." I walk back into the bedroom where Rowan hasn't moved, and who now stares at the floor.

Bright eyes meet mine as he hears me, and I tense because they're brimful of silver magic. "Where's Grayson?" he asks gruffly.

"I don't know. He left before I did." I sit on my bed and Rowan's mouth hardens. "What's wrong?"

"He left you alone? I should've stayed and protected you!" Holly walks from the bathroom and glances at me nervously as Rowan's voice rises.

"You helped Holly. That helped me."

He scowls. "Did you *at least* ask Grayson about the Petrescu attorney?"

I wince. Look how far from myself I drifted tonight— everything about this investigation left my head as the vamp took over my body and mind. I planned the evening solely to further my inquiries, and I never asked the most important question. "I didn't find a chance before he left."

"Violet!" He drags a hand through his hair in exasperation, cheeks reddening.

"On a positive note, the damage to the room helped."

"Helped us get into more shit?" he says wearily. "Seriously, Violet?"

"No. I found something else in the bedroom, hidden beneath the nightstands. The Sawyers must *really* worry about their clash with shifters. They protect themselves with warding runes." I walk over to my wall, grabbing a pen from the desk as I pass, before drawing on the corner of a paper. "This rune."

Rowan glances up. "They have witch and vamp friends?"

"Correct. But Kai told me his father doesn't like witches." I tap the pen on my lips. "They never come to the house if Sawyer's around. The rune is a simple one—most witches can create those, so could be anybody."

"You think the witch who created the rune is connected to that pendant Kai wore?" asks Rowan. "How much danger is the family in if they need all that magic?"

"Ah. But this becomes more confusing. Logan had a pendant that matched Kai's." I touch my throat. "Grayson tore it from around his neck. The talisman definitely wards against supernatural interference because I couldn't read Logan's mind."

"A warding pendant?" Rowan sits straighter.

"Logan told me he took the necklace from Wesley. Why do sons of important families possess protective talismans?"

"Good question," says Rowan as he takes a closer look.

I can't remember exactly how the pendant looked, but I scrawl an approximate copy beneath Kai's name. "Did you ever see Wesley wearing this, Holly?" I tap the paper.

Holly rises and examines the sketch. "No, but I've seen Kai wearing one a few times. I thought it was an old coin. Is it magical?" She blinks. "If that pendant protects people, I want one."

"Why?" I ask.

"Uh. For protection?"

"Nobody is remotely interested in you," I reply and return to studying the image. "You're of no significance."

"Violet," says Rowan. "Think about the words you use."

"Oh." I turn to Holly, her eyes now wet with tears, and I wince. "My apologies. I meant nobody is interested in killing you since your connection to these people and the town is tenuous."

"You could've clarified. Don't you understand how stressful this is for me? I never get into trouble and now... My parents will kill me," she says in a wavering voice.

"Infanticide as punishment for a minor crime would be rather excessive. If you believed that would happen, why help?" I ask.

She gawks. "Not literally. Why? Do parents kill misbehaving kids in your world?"

I shrug. "Probably. Some have old-fashioned views."

"*Old-fashioned*? I'm glad I'm human."

"Then I question your sanity." I step closer to my wall to add more notes. What the...? "Holly. Did you write on my wall?"

She scoffs. "No way. You get pissed these days, which is scarier than when you said nothing."

Reaching out, I rub the paper in case I'm imagining what I see. I'm not. Somebody drew a faint arrow in blue ink pointing from Rory's to Wesley's names.

"Who wrote this?" I demand and jab a finger.

"What's wrong?" asks Rowan and moves closer too.

"This! Look. I never drew that arrow between Wesley's and Rory's names."

"Are you sure?" he asks.

"Yes!" He recoils at my half-yell and Holly retreats back under her blanket.

"That doesn't make any sense," I say, jaw clenched.

"Someone invaded our room again. The same person who stole my potion."

Oh no.

I push past Rowan and kneel to pull out my trunk from beneath the bed, shaking as I place a hand on each runic ward. Intact and the potion inside. I sink back onto my heels and shove both hands into my hair, teeth grinding. "This isn't right. None of this is right. Somebody's taunting me."

"I don't like this." Holly wraps arms around herself, voice wavering again. "I don't feel safe if someone can break into our room."

"But the person didn't break in, Holly. They have a key." I glare at the mysterious arrow.

"That's even worse!"

"Right. I've decided." Rowan sits on the floor, back resting against my bed.

"What are you doing?"

"I'm not leaving you."

"You can't stay in our room!" retorts Holly.

He scowls. "I won't do anything to you. I'll sleep on the floor."

"Who exactly are you defending me from?" I ask. "Not Grayson."

"No. People with pendants that protect *them* from *you*. Ones who might look for Violet Blackwood," he retorts. "People with keys."

"Right! That's it! I'm going to Marci's," announces Holly, immediately rummaging in her wardrobe, yanking out a small black rucksack that she shoves clothes in. She grabs her blanket. "Someone walk me to Pendle house."

"The witches?" I frown.

"Yes." She tips her chin. "Marci runs the dance committee and we're close friends. *She's* not pursued by homicidal maniacs."

I chew my lip and look back to my board. Holly has no

close ties to any events, but she *is* connected to me. "How will you explain your arrival at 11pm and your distressed state?"

"I'll tell Marci you did something to my mind," she says in a wavering voice. "If that's the story we're using."

I press my lips together. "I don't know. Are you safe?"

"Marci's one of the strongest witches at Thornwood and unofficial house head girl," says Rowan. "If Holly wants to stay away from you tonight, I'd choose Pendle House over Darwin."

"You think Holly needs protecting?" I snort. "None of this concerns her. She has no connection."

"Apart from leaving with the guy who caused criminal damage at the party?" she suggests.

"I *mind-controlled* you. That's the story you're telling people, Holly. Stay here. Rowan—you can leave. Find Leif."

Holly and Rowan look at each other and he nods at her. "Violet. I agree Holly would be safer if she stays with Marci tonight."

"Ridiculous. Nobody will walk into our room and murder Holly in her bed," I retort. "Not without me noticing, since I'm sure she'll scream."

Holly squeaks and grabs her favorite plush pig. "I'm leaving."

Before I can respond, the pig is in her rucksack, and she's out of the door. "Fine. Go with Holly and stay until you're satisfied she's alright."

"Why me? She doesn't trust me."

"And I don't want to explain why I'm wandering around Pendle House," I say and gesture at my wall. "And I have to figure this out." Rowan mutters and stands to follow Holly. "Then find Leif."

"Can we wait until the morning?" he asks wearily. "I'm too tired to run through everything again. The guy's probably asleep. *Grayson* is the one you need to find."

"Not yet." I rub my forehead. "I have things to process."

And I'm not meeting Grayson until I can no longer sense my darkness close to the surface.

Chapter Twenty-Two

VIOLET

I'VE CHOSEN TO STAY NUMB OVER THE YEARS, BUT TONIGHT that feeling comes from emotions overwhelming me, not due to successfully burying them. How have I moved from total control to almost none in the space of days?

I rub my temples—the only way to cope with the chaos roaring inside me right now is to keep all my focus on solving other problems.

But what do I do about Grayson? I barely recognized myself or the way I responded to him—the girl in that room hasn't appeared for years. Last time I remotely behaved in that way, my size and age prevented too much damage to those around me. Now, the violent Violet I keep under my control can escape. Is this something the witch bond opened up? Without that, would Grayson have the same effect on me? I expect so, but my responses would not be as extreme.

Or would they? We should also investigate Rowan's theory that Grayson uses something to influence me and I'm unaware. If I bring him to one of our meetings, Rowan could see through him if this is true. Surely.

I'm staring blankly at my murder wall when I hear Rowan return. No, *sense* Rowan return before he walks in and closes the door. His energy is less tangible than earlier tonight, but still intense.

"Where's Leif?" I ask.

"Asleep. Wasn't answering his door, and I didn't think hammering and yelling would be a good idea after earlier. Kinda want to keep a low profile around Darwin house."

I turn. He's lost all color, hair a bigger mess from constantly running his hands through, but he's focusing concerned eyes on me.

"Shame we can't hunt the fools and wipe their minds," I say.

"Yeah, and track down everyone from the party. Violet. Even we don't possess enough magic between us to alter half the town's kids' minds."

"Next time I'm invited to a party, allow me to gouge my eye instead." I look back to the wall and the taunting arrow. "I should've let you investigate and stayed away myself. Social occasions aren't my forte."

Rowan stands beside me and looks at the wall too. "What happened tonight, Violet?" he asks softly.

"We found clues and also confusion?" I suggest.

"No. Why were you bleeding? What did Grayson do to you?" He's trying to keep his voice even, but the pissed edge is unmistakable.

"Nothing. Didn't you see what happened?"

"Only once everybody crowded around the door to the room. I'd sensed something wrong and ran upstairs." We keep looking at the wall and not each other. "Did somebody *else* hurt you? Those kids?"

"That's impossible," I reply evenly.

"You're not infallible."

Finally, I turn to face Rowan. Earlier, he looked flat and exhausted, now everything about him screams concern. Protection. "Grayson didn't hurt me. Neither did the humans."

"Then why are you... off? Your aura, I mean." The eyes that reflect me in more ways than one search mine, as if trying to look into my mind.

"How much do you see or sense about me without trying?" I ask stiffly.

"More than you'd like." He half-smiles. "I try to keep out, but sometimes you overwhelm me. Like now. Tell me what's wrong with you."

Moistening my lips, I look back at the tangled world I created on the wall. "Grayson saved the humans' lives tonight."

"By controlling himself? Yeah, I'm not sure I would've kept that control if I saw an aggressive guy with his hands on you."

"No, Rowan. Grayson stopped me from tearing into that guy. Everything I worried about is happening—my dark side took over tonight." I pause, but he responds with silence. "You don't know how close I came to ripping into that guy."

"You have the potion that stops your desire for human blood. You'd be okay."

"I didn't want his blood; I wanted to kill him." The silence grows intense, so I look back at his unreadable face. "I barely controlled myself. What if one day soon that part takes over?"

"The part you've caged?" he asks, and I nod. "The side you need to deal with or become engulfed by?"

"I do deal with this side of me."

"No, Violet. *Deal with* by accepting what you are, not hide and deny until you wake up and realize you've no control left."

"You don't understand," I protest.

"Yes, I do understand, since I have a badly caged part too." His little finger brushes mine, and magic flickers, but we don't look at each other.

"I've seen. That's my fault. We're bad for each other," I reply.

"Are we? Don't you understand how powerful we can be?"

"Destructive?" I ask quietly as still neither of us look away from the wall.

"If we wanted." Rowan's fingers link with mine, warm and soothing; no magic flowing, but I still tense. "I'm lying if I tell you I don't want power because I do. You think that the bond intensifies this desire, but you've calmed me."

"The magic I've seen from you is intense, Rowan," I say. "And Blackwood shadows aren't calm."

"Yes. But our bond is more than magic. For the first time, my focus shifted from what I planned to achieve alone, to caring about someone else. Thinking about someone else." His fingers grip harder as my stomach knots. "But I could take the power our bond creates and use every ounce," he says softly. "All I ever wanted was to be in control of everything."

"Why are you that desperate for power, Rowan?" I whisper. "To hurt people?"

"No. I don't want to take over, only to keep people out. Stop others using their power on me. I want people to be scared of me. Respect me."

"You don't get respect by scaring people, Rowan."

He laughs softly. "Are you sure?"

Dorian. "Is that why you want my help with a Blackwood spell?"

"I want the darkness that's inside you to bring me the shadows. If I could control them as I can the elements, nobody would touch me."

I involuntarily grip his fingers harder and look at him.

"Even Dorian never touched the shadows. I'd never agree to unleashing that magic, Rowan."

For a long moment, he says nothing, and my scalp prickles as I notice something different in his eyes. *The night with the shifters.* "You already touched the shadows. Rowan, you can't expect me to help you bring them back."

"You don't understand. We both have a darkness we struggle to control, Violet, but together we can help each other."

I pull my hand away. "To create more? No! I've spent my life denying that part of me. I'm not feeding the darkness now."

"Violet." He takes my hand again. Both hands. "To control. To let each other in and shape the darkness, rather than the dark shape us."

"If you allow the shadows into yourself and the world, they'll take over. They feed and feed on witches with desires like yours. You wouldn't stop." Rowan scoffs. "I'm serious!"

Even before the bond, I underestimated Rowan's dangerous depths but began to see his capabilities—and his threat to my father's world. *Our* world. Confusion tumbles around my mind. What am I encouraging in him as the bond tightens?

"And *I* will not feed or feed on the dark, Rowan."

"Our bond doesn't only feed the dark. If you let me in, you'll see how my soul can soothe yours." He grazes his knuckles against my cheek, drawing me into a different intensity between us. There's a familiar buzz, but this time Rowan doesn't touch the dark I worried he wants to take from me, instead a warmth flows from him.

"I will always accept what you are. I will always be here when you need," he says.

"I don't need anybody. I can't need anybody," I say, and the words stick in my throat.

"You'd spend life frightened?"

"I am not frightened of anything." I snap out of his strange influence and take a step away.

"Yes, you are. You've said this—you're frightened of yourself. Why? Because you'll become your father?" He reaches for my hand again. "You're as much your mother and you're repressing her too." I swallow the growing lump in my throat, stunned by the insight Rowan has. "Dorian and Eloise complete each other, Violet. So do we."

"No. We don't. We're not them." I can't take my eyes from his, locked with him away from my normality, and the retort comes to breathlessly.

"You can't see outside yourself, Violet. You refuse to connect. To be." He touches my cheek again. "Without that, you're a loose cannon. We both are if we're disconnected from everything." I swallow hard and shake my head. "Let me in. Please," he whispers. "This isn't all about magic and witch bonds, but I care about you, Violet. I can't even spend a day without wanting you to want me. To see me as *Rowan*—not the annoying bonded witch."

Little by little the last few days, Rowan opened a part of me I never wanted anyone to see. Not only the vampire who wanted to kill tonight, but a girl who doesn't guard her heart. The night in the rain, I almost hated that I wanted Rowan to touch and kiss me. Instead I pushed him away to prevent him taking powerful magic from our bond—power that would threaten my father and our world. I didn't want to give my magic away, and I convinced myself *that's* what stopped me.

But the truth is, I didn't want to give myself away.

On that night and for the first time, someone's touch didn't trigger my normal instinct to withdraw. This surging energy between our hands came from something more than magic and that exists deep within Rowan, a deeper connection that he tried to tell me, but I wouldn't listen. I couldn't allow myself to hear that he shares the thoughts and feelings I denied.

But I'm only one half of this situation—Rowan protected himself too with his sarcasm and teasing, his attempts at control.

Rowan's gaze flicks to my lips and back to my eyes and I'm finally unable to deny the other reason my heart speeds around him. Rowan knows and accepts what I am, and I'm drawn to him on levels I've ignored.

"I do see you as who you are, Rowan," I tell him.

"The annoying bonded witch?"

"Sometimes, but you can't help your irritating manner."

"Incorrect, I regularly practice irritating you." He smiles as I frown. "For *that* reason—*any* response from you at all means something to me."

I take a shaky breath, wrapped in the moment with him by more than the magic that I refused to share. "But I'm also the only one who *does* see the real Rowan. You hide yourself better than I do."

"Oh, yeah. I'm as unhinged as you are."

"Like meets like," I say and half-smile.

Rowan hesitantly strokes his thumb across my lips, watching the movement that sends a tingle across my face. "Undoubtedly."

Yet I also see the Rowan who cares, the guy who craves more between us, the one who wants to give himself without trying to take all of me. I've two sides I deny, and if I allow myself to connect to one, maybe I can control the other. Because within them both lies the part Eloise told me I can't deny—a natural desire for physical connection to another.

To Rowan.

I catch and hold his hand and Rowan's eyes grow wary when I tiptoe to bring our faces nearer. He's close enough that our lips feel as if they're touching, but the distance between them is a gulf. Even if I trust Rowan, do I trust myself not to succumb to the magic we'd share if I take this step?

"Don't look at me as if I'm about to bite you," I say, as the strange desire for him flutters like moths inside my belly.

"I'm more worried about you throwing me out the window if my lips get any closer," he whispers.

In answer, I softly press my mouth to his, and Rowan's response isn't what I expected. There's none. Confused, I step back to see an unexpected expression—as if I'd slapped and not kissed him.

"I took my 'don't bite witches' supplement today," I say. "Or don't you want to kiss me?"

Rowan's eyes are darker, almost gray, and although he smiles, he doesn't speak. A hand slides along my face, fingers pushing into my hair as his thumb rests on my cheek. "That's a ridiculous question, Violet Blackwood."

His lips touch mine and the warmth and softness take hold of the Violet only he sees, as more than our bond wraps around and draws me to him. Rowan kisses gently, hesitant, closing out the world for a moment.

He draws me closer until our bodies meet, as natural as the kiss. I lift a hand to Rowan's face and splay my fingers across his cheek, but the unfamiliar desire taking over my body and mind sends panic roaring through too, and I tense.

As if sensing this, Rowan breaks the kiss and presses his lips against my forehead as we stand in silence, breaths synchronizing. "I wish you understood that you were in my heart long before touching my soul, Violet."

"Don't spoil this with ridiculous platitudes," I say, my own heart refusing to calm as I grasp out for my more familiar self. "Or expect me to respond with similar words."

Rowan laughs and moves away. "You're incomparable, Violet Blackwood, and bond or no bond, I'm falling hard for you."

"Then be careful you don't hurt yourself."

I know he wasn't literal—and Rowan *knows* I know. We're both aware that despite his glimpse of this me, I won't stop hiding behind my barriers against the world. He's aware I built them to keep the world safe, but Rowan also saw more than I accept—I built walls to protect myself. And for the first time, I don't feel I need those walls all the time.

He tucks hair behind my ear, grazing heat as he brushes my neck. "I do have one request, Rowan."

"Anything."

"Don't kill anybody on my behalf."

"I don't intend to bring you the heads of our enemies, but duly noted."

"Or their hearts," I add.

"There's only one heart I want to give you." He smirks, eyes glinting.

"Rowan, please stop there. The window is close by."

"I know. I'm just the annoying witch pushing your buttons." He leans closer. "Although I'd appreciate you not taking the heart-giving literally. I'd rather keep that inside my chest."

The odd sensation that's moved from a fluttering to a swarm inside me grows, a response I would never dream of having to the irritating witch who constantly outsmarts me.

But isn't that the whole reason *why* I respond to Rowan as I do?

"Agreed. I'd rather you stayed alive," I reply.

"Is that a half-hearted way of telling me you care?"

"I kissed you Rowan Willowbrook. Does that not tell you enough?"

"No. Remind me." Again, that damn smirk.

I narrow my eyes. "I have more important things to do than involve myself in physical entanglements. I've a lot of issues to resolve after tonight's events."

Rowan laughs. "As always. Another time then?"

I attempt to consider the situation, but I've reached a point where my mind has abandoned carefully considered logic. Rowan's right, we're not a problem to solve; Rowan and

I are something to work on. Dipping my toes in intimacy is illogical to me, but I would like a closeness with Rowan. The contradiction spins my head.

"Another time," I say. "Although I can't specify when."

Rowan draws me into an encompassing hug, and I almost protest we've ended our moments of physical and emotional affinity, but there's a comfort in the protective arms and warmth from his body I've never desired. Somewhat ironically, his clean scent reminds me of the earth after a thunderstorm, and I slide my arms around Rowan's waist to return his affection.

For a moment.

Chapter Twenty-Three

VIOLET

Rowan stayed in my room last night—further away than he'd prefer. He isn't dumb enough to attempt to climb into bed with me, although Rowan was snoring in Holly's long before I stopped poring over my notes and scrawling frustrated thoughts on paper. I can't spend time considering the change in my relationship with Rowan. I'll allow myself time to expend mental energy on that later.

Is the arrow to indicate Rory killed Wesley? Why? Instructed by the shifters—Viggo? If that's true, who killed Rory?

I send Rowan away to find Leif and instruct him to meet in the library after breakfast, and he wanders off laughing to himself about 'business as usual'. I'm confused by both his words and amusement?

I don't even make it to breakfast since I'm intercepted before I manage to cross campus. Of course, because life can never be simple in this world I'm thrust into. If I ignored instructions to attend a meeting at the administration rooms, that'll lead to more repercussions when I want the day to run more smoothly than the last.

We need to meet. To discuss. To plan.

To find Grayson.

Have the Thornwood guys who attempted to intimidate me told authorities that Violet Blackwood, in turn, threatened to kill people who upset her? Thus, confirming my reputation.

Or is this something more serious? Please let Kai be alive.

I reach the front of the academy building where a single prestige black car is parked. Odd since the only cars parked on 'Violet is in trouble days' are the detectives and my father's. Dorian must've used blood runes to travel, and the detectives aren't here since neither car is parked beside the Audi. I scrutinize the personalized plate: SAWYER1.

Interesting. Perhaps I won't need to wait long to meet the man.

I stomp up the steps into the echoing entrance hall and along the now familiar route towards the headteachers' offices.

Only when I reach the administrative part of the academy does something strike me. There's no presence from Dorian or Eloise in the surroundings. Or Rowan. Why only me? But as I move towards the waiting room, I'm aware there's someone familiar who's definitely in the vicinity.

Grayson sits on one of the sofas, an ankle crossed over his other knee and hands linked behind his head. Wound free, emerald eyes bright. As he holds my gaze, everything from last night tumbles into my mind, and I'm sure he notices the switch in my heart rate.

"Where did you go last night?" I ask, voice hushed.

"Away from you."

"Where?"

Grayson unlinks his hands and sits forward. "We need to talk."

155

I push my tongue against my top teeth. "Oh, we most certainly do. Such as you telling me who Josef Petrescu is."

His cocky smile fades. "What?"

The office door opens, and Mrs. Lorcan walks out. "You're both fortunate," she says quietly.

"In what respect?" I ask. "As my current location and your face suggest otherwise."

She frowns. "Mr. Sawyer hasn't immediately pressed charges."

"He's here?" asks Grayson.

"Does that concern you?" I ask pointedly, but he looks away.

"Why? Would you prefer the police?" asks Mrs. Lorcan.

"I haven't caught up with my detective friends for a few days. They might jump at the chance as I expect they miss my sparkling personality and quick wit," I reply.

She glares at me. "Mr. Sawyer wanted to deal with the matter privately. Violet—keep quiet when he speaks to you both, otherwise he's likely to change his mind."

"But I always have so much to say, Mrs. Lorcan."

Her intensely pissed expression grows harsher.

"Where's Logan and his buddies who attacked Violet?" asks Grayson.

"Attacked Violet?" Mrs. Lorcan says incredulously. "And how exactly would they manage that? I'm more bothered about *your* attack." She jabs a finger at him. "Such behavior is exactly that which threatens your place at Thornwood, Grayson Petrescu."

"Technically, not, since this didn't happen on campus," I put in, only to be ignored.

Grayson pulls a non-committal face. "The guy made me pissed."

She clenches her jaw and straightens her shirtsleeves. "Let's see what Mr. Sawyer has to say about the situation."

Again, a look at me and the suggestion that I say little. As she ushers us inside, she surely knows how unlikely that is.

Christopher Sawyer fills the room in the way many supes do, but few humans, apart from those with a presence that comes from a large ego and prestigious life. Although his isn't magical, Sawyer's years of influence over people created a person who many humans would never mess with.

I'm close enough to see him clearly this time, and Christopher Sawyer's face appears too unlined to be father to Kai, unless he was a young father or ages well. Momentarily, the thought he might be a supe crosses my mind, since that would explain a lot, but he's a hundred percent human. Probably injects bizarre substances into his face.

His close-cropped, neat graying hair betrays his age, while his gray tailored suit and expensive gold watch betray his wealth. Sawyer's face gives away nothing as he leans back in the leather desk chair, sitting as if this is his office and not Mr. Willis's.

He gestures at two chairs opposite the mahogany desk, but neither of us sit. Is he deliberately silent in an attempt to intimidate us? Because he won't succeed.

"Where's Logan?" I ask.

"Hello, Violet. I've heard much about you."

"I expect so. I'm a popular topic of conversation currently."

He smiles. "And you. Grayson Petrescu." Hmm. Sawyer doesn't sound as if he's met Grayson before. "I hear you involved yourself in last night's unfortunate incident."

"I helped Violet against an attack," he says evenly.

"From what I've heard, Violet doesn't need anybody's protection." He taps his manicured fingers on the table. "Almost as if you both created a distraction for some reason."

"Excuse me?" I retort. "The assholes cornered and threatened me. No, I don't need protection, but they would've needed protection from *me* if I'd reacted in the way they desired. Grayson merely interrupted the situation."

"And then he threatened an academy student with death?" Sawyer leans back in his seat. "Yes, I've spoken to Logan and his friends already."

Grayson shrugs. "Like I said, I was pissed with him."

"Now, I understand that there's a third party involved—Rowan Willowbrook—but his criminal damage was to other children's property. Yours was to my house."

"A broken glass door?" I ask. "I can arrange to fix that."

Sawyer leans forward again. "No. The damage caused by the fighting your actions triggered. A lot of damage to my lounge room and furniture, with several other rooms ransacked."

"What?" I ask sharply. "We never started a fight—ours was personal with Logan and his cretins." And as I left via the balcony, I jumped to a quiet side of the house and didn't pass through the party again. I'd most certainly had enough of company by that point. "The other fight has nothing to do with us."

"While you distracted people with your fight, something valuable disappeared from my home." Sawyer sits forward and rests his forearms on the table. "Who stole from me?"

"What was stolen?" I ask, and he arches a brow. "I never took anything."

"No, because you were the distraction, correct? Most phones were tampered with and destroyed, but my security cameras caught images of you leaving via the balcony." He slants his head. "Who took the item?"

This item can't be large if a security camera picked us up without anything in our hands, yet we're still accused.

"With respect," says Grayson, "if we don't know what the item is, how can we answer?"

Sawyer shifts around in his seat. "You allegedly threatened to kill someone last night. I suggest you cooperate with me."

"Yes. *Allegedly* threatened to kill," I put in.

"Ah yes, no footage, but many witnesses." Sawyer gives a tight smile. "Like you *allegedly* provoked and attacked those poor boys at the party, Miss Blackwood."

I clench my jaw. Naturally, the story's twisted in the human assholes' favor.

"What's missing?" I ask bluntly.

"Jewelry taken from the safe in my office." He narrows his eyes. "A well-secured safe that would take magic to open quickly."

"I'm sorry, but we know nothing about that," says Grayson, looking him straight in the eyes. "Perhaps the police could watch out for the item. If it's valuable, the thief might try to sell to someone?"

"Worthless."

"You said valuable," I hit back.

A long look. "Sentimental value. Do I need to call in your friends Rowan and Holly, or would you like to admit what you did? I understand that both would wish to avoid expulsion or criminal charges."

"This is crazy," says Grayson, "we never touched your things."

Ignoring Grayson, Sawyer stands. "You have a problem, my young friends. If you return the item to me, I won't press charges about the criminal damage to my home, nor involve your friends." I eye him suspiciously. "Kai often invites half the town's kids to the house, *anybody* could've caused this damage, and I wouldn't know exactly who. But I may 'discover' the culprits, if necessary."

Jewelry? Sentimental value? I don't think so. Is this another magical trinket?

"Again, what item?" I ask.

"If you possess it, you'll know."

"And if we don't? How the hell can we return it?" blurts Grayson.

His eyes turn to Grayson. "I have a powerful attorney."

As Grayson's look darts away, Sawyer flicks a look to me too, but I stare back, unmoved.

"I won't tell you who I have that's powerful," I say evenly. "And he doesn't appreciate false accusations against his daughter."

"Ah yes. Your recent murderous rampage around town. And last night, a fight with my son. If something happens to him, I won't hesitate to use my influence and you'll be charged for all three murders."

His influence? More than an academy head's because Mr. Willis couldn't ensure my incarceration for his son's death.

"Why do you think something will happen to Kai?" I ask. Sawyer regards me but says nothing. "Are you aware that Kai intends to attend Rory's wake?"

"I've instructed him not to attend, and he understands there'll be consequences if he does. Are *you* attending?"

"Me? Good grief, no." Yes. "Are many from town going? Dignitaries such as yourself?"

He trains a steady gaze on me. "I don't discuss my movements with you. The town's business is none of yours."

"Apart from when you're all accusing me of murder?" I suggest. "I have no reason to kill Kai."

Grayson clears his throat and I clamp my lips together in case I add my thoughts about this arrogant human and his son.

"Twenty-four hours." Sawyer stands. He walks towards the door and yanks the handle, opening it and then holding the edge. "Good luck with your search. Off you go, kiddies."

I'm practically grinding my teeth as we walk through the academy away from Kai's father.

Chapter Twenty-Four

VIOLET

AM I SURPRISED OR UNSURPRISED WHEN GRAYSON BOLTS THE moment we walk from our meeting with Sawyer? I pull out my phone and send Rowan a quick message about what happened and reassure him that we'll make our library meeting, but an hour later.

Then I set about looking for the vampire who I'd prefer to avoid. His response when I mentioned Josef Petrescu adds to my suspicion. Until I discover if he's related to this Petrescu, I can't move on—with the investigation or what happened last night.

In the room at the party, the humans already provoked me and brought out the bloodthirsty vampire, and that's why I lost of control of myself around Grayson. Right. Yes. Such a response won't happen again.

How stupid am I if I believe that? My vampire state intensified the reaction that triggers every time the guy comes near me—and Grayson knows. He shares the same desire for more, and although the blinded lust for his blood overcame me, something more happened. Is this what Eloise means about blood and intimacy going hand in hand? Because when Grayson touched me, my own blood ran hotter, and I wanted him to press me to the wall and kiss me.

Good grief. No. I wanted that because biting his lip would be the perfect, easiest access to his blood. But even as I picture that, the image of a kiss is stronger than the bite.

This is bad.

Very, very bad.

I head through the academy to Sheridan House wing. He might return to his room. There's no way I'd enter said room, but I could drag him out of the place.

I've no need since Grayson's sitting on a bench at the bottom of the steps that spiral up and around to the vampires' accommodation, and he stands when I approach. I stop in front of him, close enough to speak, but far enough to resist his scent befuddling my senses. For moments we stand in silence, each wary of the other.

"Violet," he says quietly.

"Grayson."

How many times have we met in this way? Several, but never with such knowledge about each other heavy in the air.

"You ran again," I say. "Why?"

"Can't keep away, huh?" he asks.

Neither of us move.

"I'd like to finish our earlier conversation."

"You seem calmer," he bats back. "I hope you left everybody's throats intact last night."

"Yours is."

He chuckles and moves another step closer. "I might entertain what you want if you've more control over yourself now."

Grayson knows what he's doing and so do I—if he recreates the same response in me as last time, on his terms, he's the one in control. I can't lie about his effect on me ever again, but the call of Grayson's blood isn't the reason I sought him.

And control is about to pass to me. "Is Josef Petrescu closely related to you?"

"Why?" he asks sharply, casual stance turning defensive in the blink of an eye.

"Answer the question," I say stiffly. "You responded as if you knew him, before Mrs. Lorcan rudely interrupted."

Grayson's eyes glint and I prepare myself to catch him if he decides to run. "He's my uncle."

My heart lodges in my throat.

Uncle?

Closer than expected. And how close are they? "Do you see him often?"

Grayson's alarm leaves his mind wide open to me, but as I reach inside, he slams down a barrier. "Out of my head, Violet. I see him occasionally when he visits."

My pulse continues to race. "At the academy?"

"No. In town."

"When he visits Christopher Sawyer?" More silence. I move into the gap he's left between us and tip my head, hoping to see more than lies in his eyes.

"Why does this feel like an interrogation?"

I swallow as his blood rises closer to his skin. "He's an attorney, right?" Grayson nods. "The Sawyer family's attorney."

"Is he?" Grayson looks at my mouth and tugs his lip with his teeth, and I blink away the deliberate distraction. "We don't talk much and certainly not about his daily life."

I hold my ground. "Do you know if your uncle was in town the nights Wesley and Rory died?"

I hear nothing but my heart and his as I wait for Grayson's reply. Images of last night intrude again and I'm half-convinced Grayson is planting them to wash away my questions. "This is the point I could lie to you,

Violet. Because I've never spoken to anybody about him before."

"You don't want to tell me the truth?" Grayson's face betrays nothing. "Will you answer or not?"

"Walk with me, Violet."

"Where?"

He stands over me, and even though he isn't bleeding this time, the scent from his skin is enough to trigger my unwanted response. "Don't look at me in that way. I won't assault you." He lowers his voice. "Or are you worried that *you* might assault *me*? Violet, you attacked me last night, wanting my blood, and now ask me to tell you my secrets."

"I didn't attack you."

"I know. Because I stopped you. Next time ask nicely."

Closing my eyes, I take a steady breath. "Answer my question."

"If I tell you about my uncle, you have to promise that whatever you find out about him, you inform me," Grayson replies, dropping his teasing tone.

How would Rowan feel about Grayson involved in our investigating? Because he might not have the choice. "If I believe your story."

"You probably won't." He rubs two fingers across his lips. "I'd rather not speak to you about this where someone could pass by or hear."

I nod, but he's already walked away. I follow Grayson from the building, and we head towards the cloisters. The grounds are empty apart from straggling students wandering to the classes I've no intention of attending, and I happily escape the warm day as we stand behind the walls.

Grayson sits on a bench and looks up at me. "Did you steal anything from Sawyer?"

"No. Did you?"

"Why would I? Or rather, why would Sawyer accuse you?"

"I'm not discussing my investigations with you until I'm clear that you're not involved."

Grayson's expression shadows. "Listen to my story and then make up your mind."

I shrug and wave a hand, even though I'm most certainly not nonchalant about this.

He sighs. "That first day when you were rude about my family name? You were half-right. I'm supposed to represent the changed Petrescu family, but I have our level of self-control—hardly any. I hurt somebody."

"I heard. You left campus but the academy let you return even though you assaulted a student. Why would they?"

"I didn't assault anybody. Everything happened with consent, but I went too far." He pauses. "And you know how easily some of us can lose control, Violet Blackwood."

"I'm not like you," I snap. "Stop trying to distract me."

He blows air into his cheeks. "After the… event, my uncle asked my parents if I could spend time with him."

"Why?"

"I'm not going into full details, but let's just say we went away for a few days, and he punished me. The academy allowed me to return if my uncle promised to 'keep an eye' on me. I'm back, but my punishment isn't over, Violet. I'm forced to meet him several times a week to check if I've… strayed." I frown. "That's the blood you saw on me. My blood from his 'treatment'."

I edge sideways. "Why do they punish you? Because you've 'strayed' and attacked people?"

His mouth becomes a thin line. "No. As a reminder that worse will happen if I do. My uncle and his friends… did things to try and desensitize me. I've no potion like you and I enjoy—enjoyed—that side of my nature."

"And you still do?" I ask cautiously.

"No. I only want your blood."

I wrap my arms around myself, mind reeling, but he won't

draw me into that place where we secretly exist together. "Is this true, Grayson?" I ask.

"About wanting your blood?"

"No," I say crossly. "About your uncle."

"Yes. Why would I make up shit like that?"

Because you're told to? "If this is true, your uncle was in town when the guys died."

"Yeah." He folds his arms. "I asked him about the deaths, but Josef claims he wasn't involved."

"All Petrescu elders hate my father and his council. This is an opportunity for them." I try to catch his thoughts, but they're dulled and closed to me. "What do you know about your uncle and the Sawyers?"

He scoffs. "Nothing. I barely know anything about Josef's life, even if I'm very familiar with his teeth and fists."

"Do *you* believe your uncle isn't involved?"

"Honestly? I don't know. He is interested in you though. Josef asked me to get close to Dorian's daughter." My eyes go wide. "I'd decided to keep away instead, but looks like we're irresistible to each other."

Grayson's light humor does nothing to take away the heaviness surrounding the new facts. "Why are you telling me this, Grayson? Won't they 'discipline' you if they knew?"

"Because if my family is implicated, I don't want you to accuse me too."

"What do they want to know about me? Because there're no secrets in my life. You may've noticed I'm upfront about everything."

Grayson studies me again. "And I'm being upfront with you. I want to help."

"You just told me your uncle asked you to spy on me," I say tersely.

"And what if I told you I'd spy on them for you?"

"These men hurt and torture you."

"And I don't want them to hurt you, Violet."

Despite his softer look, I harden. "Yet you want my blood as you casually and unsubtly mentioned?"

"Oh, I want your blood, as you want mine, but not via coercion."

"There's an echo of the past here that makes me uncomfortable, Grayson, and not only your name. Dorian originally wanted my mother's blood for the power it would give him."

He scoffs. "I'm not interested in power. Any power. I'm interested in protecting myself when shit goes down, and if the murders involve my uncle, I'll help against him."

I'm registering changes in my heartbeat frequently in recent days, particularly around the guys, or in moments that interfere with my ability to process what I hear. Like now.

What did I expect from Grayson's explanation? A secret hemia society that fight amongst themselves? That he tricked me and the blood on his face came from human or witches fighting back? Even when suspicions solidified once we discovered a Petrescu connection, I never for a moment thought of *this* scenario.

"Do you believe my story?" he asks.

"Show me." I tap the side of my head. "Memories."

"No." His response comes quickly, a hint of panic.

"Then I won't believe you. Not fully."

"Your boyfriend can take a look."

"Rowan is not my boyfriend," I retort. One kiss. *But so much more, Violet.*

"Sure, he isn't," he says and laughs. "If Rowan sees that I'm telling the truth, will you accept that I intend to help you?" Grayson crosses his arms. "Because he will see everything I told you."

"Very well, but I don't understand why you won't allow *me* to look."

"Reasons," he says stiffly. "So, can I join your gang?"

"I don't have a gang. That implies I'm part of a clique within the student body."

Grayson shakes his head. "Can I join your group of followers to discuss this with them?"

"My assistants."

This time he bursts out laughing. "Oh, man. Those poor guys."

"You extend your sympathy, yet you want to join them?" I sigh. "You're an odd person."

"Uh huh."

"Okay. There's one more question before I agree." I watch his face carefully. "Have you entered my room without permission?"

He chuckles. "No. I'm waiting for when I do have permission." I scowl. "No, Violet. I have not. Why?"

"No reason. I'm meeting Rowan and Leif at the library. Come with me."

"Because you're allowing me into your mysterious circle?" he calls as I walk away.

No. Because I'd rather keep an eye on you before you disappear again.

Chapter Twenty-Five

ROWAN

WHICH PART OF LAST NIGHT COUNTS AS THE CRAZIEST? Because there's quite the choice, but the conversation and kiss with Violet wipes out everything else. Her growing acceptance of an *us* allows a closeness that matters more than a kiss, an end to the evening that I never expected when I walked out the door to the disastrous party.

Where do we go now? Wherever, we're facing a slow journey, but that kiss pulled me off the course in life I planned and shouldn't follow.

I hope.

I'm stuck between a calmness from Violet's acceptance and also the remaining desire for her on every level. If she's more open around me, that'll help, but Violet's changes won't happen overnight. One day at a time. If we solve these murders, she'll have energy to put elsewhere, and hopefully we'll become part of that 'elsewhere'.

The newer edge from connecting to her Blackwood magic adds to the high I get from her presence and encourages a power I've reached for but never quite grasped. The spell to permanently protect myself—and Leif—from harm is within my grasp. Once Violet agrees and understands that I don't want to take control of everything.

The Blackwood shadows can't be that uncontrollable; Violet's concerned about something that'll never happen.

Unsurprisingly, last night might be a figment of my imagination considering how Violet's responding to me today —no differently and back in investigative mode. What did I expect? Hand holding? Smiles and subtle looks between us?

Man, we're a long way from that. Any other girl and I might've taken a chance at a more than a kiss, but if Violet had pushed me away, or the act pushed her away, I'd be on the other side of the chasm between us again. Probably the other side of town, she would've blasted me so far. I'm not risking that.

Why wasn't I called into the meeting this morning? Violet explained what happened and I'm suspicious about Sawyer's decision to target her and Grayson. Still, my involvement means he has something over me too and that could be up his sleeve, ready to pull out if he wants me yanked into line. That human's influence on the town and his links to the Petrescus and witches scream danger to me.

Violet finally spoke to Grayson earlier and didn't tell me anything apart from Josef is Grayson's uncle, which set my distrust spiraling further. Then she told me to reserve judgement until I hear the full story, and so Grayson's invited to our library meeting.

He has secrets, and I'm now positive that Grayson's uncle is involved. Is Grayson?

But, as agreed, I'll listen to the vamp's explanation.

He's sitting on the edge of the desk, his feet on a seat as we wait for Leif. Violet wanders away to check the bookshelves and our silence becomes more noticeable as time passes.

I've never disliked Grayson; I've no reason to. We barely interact beside sharing some classes, the guy once popular with a lot of girls. The reason's obvious if you look at him— attractive, with the hemia charm ready to unleash at a moment's notice. I've seen him lap up attention from girls in the past, but none go near him anymore—his 'overenthusiasm' left trust issues across the academy students and staff. Was his new vigilante status an attempt to make amends?

Violet's responses to him don't match her natural wariness around people, and although I'm fully aware powerful female witches surround themselves with consorts, they rarely choose vampires.

She's certainly caught Grayson's attention. Hell, the guy looks at her as if just minutes in her company completes his day. Better than looking at her as if he wants to pin her to the bookshelves and sink his teeth into her. I chuckle to myself, imagining how hard she'd hit him, magically or otherwise.

"You and Violet," he says eventually. "Together?"

I laugh. "Do you think anybody could be 'together' with Violet?"

He flicks his fingers in her direction. "Could've said the same about you and anybody, Rowan." I scowl. "Then it's a witch thing? You and her? You're together a lot."

"Yeah. A witch thing." I tap the edge of the table and study him. "I know you're interested in Violet too."

His emerald eyes are unreadable. "She's an interesting girl."

"That's not what I mean. Violet tells me everything."

"The blood 'issue'?" I nod, thin-lipped. "Am I stepping on toes, Rowan?" His scrutiny continues. "Want me to back off?"

I rub my lips. Do I? Yes, but not because I'm jealous, as Violet sometimes accuses me. Because although she's no typical girl, this blood lust could see her falling for a guy who could hurt her on a number of levels. "I'm keeping Violet close because I don't want anything to happen to her. She's a tendency to do and say things that cause her trouble."

"Yeah, the girl could use a few more social skills. And a filter." I can't help but share a smile—he's been a 'victim' of Violet's personality too. "But I feel the same way, Rowan. I want to protect, not hurt her. You saw that last night."

"Are you serious?" Violet now stands with a book in one hand, looking at us as if we're insane. "Protect me? Who from?"

"Yourself," says Grayson casually, and my eyes widen at his blunt response.

"As if I'd hurt myself," she retorts. "My spells never backfire, and I heal quickly."

Again, I exchange a glance with Grayson and our link suddenly becomes apparent. We've all the time in the world for this girl who needs teaching how to become part of it, and a matching desire to keep her safe. Although, Grayson's crystal clear that's not the only desire we both have.

This three-way connection could be interesting and I'm unsure if in a good or bad way, especially if I find any hint Grayson will hurt Violet. Care for her? Be someone she goes to? Fine—but once he's proved himself. He did step in last night, but whatever happened upset Violet. I didn't press the issue, more concerned about Violet's shared fears about her darker side.

That, I will help with.

"Where's Leif?" Violet asks as she places the book on the table. There's no title printed on the front, so I flick the cover open. Uh oh. Vampire families' history.

"Late, as usual," I reply.

"Fine. We'll start without him. Grayson—tell Rowan everything that you told me, and Rowan tell Grayson what we've found."

"Yes, ma'am," I say, and Grayson grins in agreement.

"Excuse me?" she asks and slams the book cover closed.

Her fingers graze against mine and jolts her magic through me; Violet purses her lips but says nothing.

Grayson says plenty. Too much.

I'm horrified by Grayson's story and how casual he is about his experiences, but mixed in with that I worry that Grayson's connection to Josef Petrescu is more than he admits. He's midway through the story when Leif rocks up, nodding his hello and pulling out a chair.

"What have I missed?" He lowers his massive frame onto the seat.

"Grayson's explanation why he walks around covered in blood the nights people die," says Violet and looks up from where she's perusing the book. "And that Josef is his uncle, is also sadistic, and wants him to spy on me."

"Oh?" Leif replies and I relay the story. "Oh. Dude, that's not good."

Grayson half-smiles at Leif's understatement. "Rowan doesn't fully believe me. I can tell."

Violet barely looks at Grayson and sits furthest from him. Did anything else happen between them earlier, such as discussing their 'issue' from last night? I'm uneasy that Violet's convinced she would've hurt or even killed one of the kids at the party, but Grayson could behave as badly. Easily. She talks of our potential to devour each other's darkness and become dangerous. How are Grayson and Violet any different?

Violet glances up again, finger on the book to hold her place. "Grayson agreed to allow you into his memories. No idea why *you* since he won't let me."

"I expect the guy doesn't want you to see him looking weak," says Leif, and Grayson's jaw hardens. "Gray, we're fighting forces hard to beat here. Believe me, I know."

Grayson slants his head. "Family troubles too?"

"Yeah, you could say that."

"Do you trust me?" I ask Grayson as I sit forward, preparing to reach into his mind.

Grayson tips his chin in acknowledgement and shifts around so he's facing me. "Go ahead. Take a look. Just don't freak out."

"As if I would. You told us the story. I'll only confirm the details as I see them."

"And I'll ensure you do, Rowan." His disconcerting eyes meet mine. "All of them."

I'm vaguely smug Grayson's allowing me into his mind until I'm confronted by what's inside. Does Grayson deliberately choose moments in his memories that are likely to horrify me the most? Violet wasn't joking about the uncle and his friends' sadistic nature. Grayson's eyes remain on mine the whole time, and Leif glances between us. I must look pale because acid builds in my mouth, my stomach heaving.

"Did you tell Violet—"

"Not everything," he interrupts. "But I hope you saw enough to know why there's no fucking way I'd help that man."

They killed Grayson.

I swallow down the bile. The bastards tortured this guy until they broke him, and he lost enough blood that he died. And a dead vampire who returns to life starved of blood... I moisten my lips. The imprisonment. Taunting.

Grayson shared his anguish and pain with the memories, and I struggle to associate that guy and the one here now, who's showing no outward sign of what he experienced.

"Do you trust him now, Rowan?" asks Violet.

"Can you explain about the coat, Gray?" I ask.

"What the fuck? Wasn't what you saw enough? I know nothing about a coat," he replies and looks at Violet. "I explained to Violet the reason you saw me near his body in your spell. Do you want to check for that in my mind too?"

"No, he doesn't," says Violet.

Old Rowan would argue that Grayson could be brainwashed since they've desensitized him, but the hatred engulfing his mind isn't fake. He hides the true effect this had on him well, but the emotion is there, and I've never sensed abhorrence or fear that great. This horror isn't something he'd easily create to trick us—only someone who's experienced that level of brutality could feel what I sensed.

How can Grayson walk this earth carrying that with him? How can he bear to return to these men time after time?

"You think that I'm weak," Grayson says tersely. "Because I go back for more."

"No, you don't have a real choice; they'd hunt you," I say hoarsely, looking at him through new eyes.

There's a world outside mine that I've never comprehended. One distant to my own, made greater by the focus on myself and magic. Nothing touched me, so why would I care? Compared to Leif and Grayson, I'm exactly what Leif's called me over the years on the rare times we've argued. A privileged asshole.

I'm the youngest of four, who keeps his head down at the academy and stays away from my parents' scrutiny. The advantage of being the baby of the family? My brothers made the mistakes before me, and I learned to hide mine. Once my parents dealt with three teens, they left the fourth alone because he didn't cause trouble.

No, not yet.

I blink from my thoughts. Everybody's looking at me with expectation. "Violet, Grayson clearly hates the man and everything he showed me backs up his story. Grayson isn't working with his uncle."

He grits his teeth. "But I'll end them, Rowan. Dorian's council is so fucking careful not to appear 'anti-Petrescu' that they overlook things. If Dorian knew—"

"And he will," Violet doesn't look up. Is she listening or

reading the book? "For now, focus. We need to plan; I'm shifting focus to Sawyer and his 'business' connections to the Petrescus." I side glance Grayson; his face betrays nothing. "Find the witches Sawyer's involved with. Discover who has access to my room."

I rest back in my seat. "And find out what was stolen from the house."

"He's working with witches, for sure," says Grayson.

"We need to know if there're any connections between Rory and Wesley apart from the pendant," adds Leif.

"Oh, yeah. That." Grayson shoves a hand in his jeans pocket and pulls out a chain, holding it up and dangling the pendant in the air.

Chapter Twenty-Six

ROWAN

"You had this and never said?" asks Violet, and snatches it from him.

"You never asked," he replies.

I close my eyes, praying for him after that comment.

"You and Rowan should be best friends," she retorts. "You have a lot in common."

"Yeah—you." He nods at me. "Right, Rowan?"

I hold my hands up. "Keep me out of this."

Violet drops the chain onto the table and we all peer at the talisman. "Go on, Rowan," says Grayson. "Use your magic but try to get the right answer this time."

"What do you think a warding talisman protects the most?" I ask tersely.

"The wearer?" asks Grayson.

"Itself," I reply. "These talismans have a tendency to injure witches who use spells on them."

"He's correct," says Violet. "But can you recognize any of the runes or letters on the pendant, Rowan?"

Carefully, I pick up the talisman, ensuring I don't touch the thing with magic and squint at the tiny black markings. "Some match the ones you copied from the book, Violet."

Eyes widening, she snatches the pendant and peers at it. "Then the code is a spell, like we thought?"

"One older than either of us knows," I say.

"And someone inside the academy wrote that spell in one of the books." Violet pulls out her phone and compares the images. "Is this a spell for protection or something else?"

"We need to keep this and compare. I'm not holding onto the pendant in case I'm injured," I say.

Violet nudges it towards Leif. "I think you should take this."

"Why?"

"If this is a protective spell, you can leave the academy and not worry about people hurting or taking you." Her eyes glint, as they do when she believes she's found the perfect solution.

"Why would I need to leave campus?" he asks.

"We're going to Rory's wake."

I choke at her simple, firm decision. "We had this discussion. No."

"I don't believe that was a discussion, per se, Rowan. Rather, you believing I'll bow to your wishes. I'm going. If anything, to ensure there's not another murder to pin on me."

"By being in the vicinity at the time?" My voice rises as Grayson and Leif look at each other. "You're sometimes stupid, considering how smart you are."

Grayson takes a sharp breath, and Violet's eyes darken. "Do you want Kai to die? Someone else? Something bad will happen at that wake." She looks to Grayson. "Is your uncle in town?"

"No. I would've heard from him. He never misses a chance to torture me." Grayson speaks with derision, but there's no doubt he's using the correct word.

Violet's jaw tightens. "After today, you need to speak to my father about your uncle, Grayson."

Grayson's whole body goes rigid. "What? No. We can't cause trouble without proof."

"Tell Dorian what he did to you. The whole story."

"Not yet, Violet. Dorian will lose his shit and cause trouble. He'll accuse me of attending the academy as a spy. A threat to you." Grayson rubs a hand across his forehead. "No."

"And I shall correct him if that occurs. Not you, but somebody in the academy isn't genuine," says Violet. "Someone stole from me. Drew the runes in Wesley's room. The arrow. What next?"

"Which is why Dorian wouldn't believe me," urges Grayson. "The Petrescu at the academy—obvious candidate."

"Let's focus on today," Leif interrupts as the tension throws us off course.

"Where do we start to unravel this?" I slump back in my seat.

"Has there ever been conflict between the Sawyers and the academy?" asks Violet.

"Not that I'm aware of. Maybe with the supernatural council?" I suggest.

"Dorian keeps out of human business unless he's dragged into something."

"Like now," says Leif.

"Ugh." Violet hits a palm against her head. "I hate this puzzle."

"The pieces are beginning to slot together." I suggest.

Badly and some forced, but we will get there.

Violet drops into a thoughtful silence for a while, picking up and twirling the pendant to look closer as her brow tugs. *Cute.* Once again, her eyes brighten, and she turns to Leif.

"Leif. I need to dig deeper into your mind for your

missing memories. I'm sure you've plenty in your head that I can sort through, perhaps put some of this jigsaw together."

"You've tried," he replies cautiously.

"Yes. If we go back to the scene, that might help?"

Leif falls silent, then shakes hair from his face. "I'm not sure I want someone to dig right inside and know everything in my head."

"In case you did kill?" she asks bluntly.

"Kind of. But other things. Thoughts are private, Violet." He squeezes his eyes closed. "But we need to, don't we?"

"Like I said, I'm concerned about the wake and Kai's life if he attends without the pendant. If he dies, that will be disastrous for me and the stability of our world."

"And for Kai?" I suggest.

"Yes. Him too."

"Why so convinced Kai will die?" asks Grayson.

"Our argument and his connections. His family. Sawyer's comments." She leans towards Leif. "Please, Leif. I promise not to invade your personal thoughts. There might be a way to piece together those memories and we've no time."

He stares at his hands, and my spirits sink. Nobody likes to leave their minds open to another. I understand, but wish he did too, because this is crucial. We have to at least try.

"If I look into your memories, then we'll know which others are involved," she says. "Won't that help you?"

Leif blows air into his cheeks and stares at his hands. "Alright. But if I killed Wes…" His throat bobs.

"You didn't," I say. "Your presence wasn't near him when we used the psychometry spell."

Violet smiles. "Yes! So, there's nothing to worry about. You won't show me anything that threatens you. Then, we can go to the wake armed with more information."

I rub my forehead. Whatever new link we made last night, this girl still won't listen to anybody but herself.

And I doubt that'll ever change.

Chapter Twenty-Seven

LEIF

I HAVEN'T RETURNED TO THIS PART OF THE WOODS SINCE THE night I visited with Rowan, searching for any items he could use a spell on. The night we met Violet searching too, and she looked at me with obvious suspicion. On the night Wes died, I told Rowan I've no memory of those hours, but the scratches and bleeding were more than when I fought with Viggo. We both knew something happened, and as always, Rowan agreed to help.

As everything happened in the gloom created by the woods that night, I struggle to find the exact spot in the afternoon daylight, so I pause close to where Kirsten found Wesley. White tea lights mingle with the bouquets at the makeshift shrine beneath the tree, now fading over time, now mourners no longer visit. As with the last time I stood here, nausea churns my stomach. What if I did kill Wes?

Violet's mind reading will hopefully find me an answer this time.

Grayson and Rowan accompany us—Rowan, since Violet

needs his magic to create the strongest spell and Grayson because he insists on staying involved now. Does Gray think if he stays with us, we can't accuse him if anything else happens? I don't know the guy well, but I'm in tune with people's vibes and Gray's matches his words. When I mentioned this to Violet, she nodded but wanted to know what vibes are because everybody speaks about them.

Amusing. Of course, Violet would never pick up on people's auras or energy. Or she didn't—I'm gaining the impression that she's recognizing peoples' responses more.

A breeze whips through the clearing and ruffles hair into my eyes as I turn to Violet. "What do we do now?" I ask.

"Sit here and shut up."

Grayson coughs out an amused laugh and Rowan nods at me. "I'll sit down and shut up too."

"Why is that funny?" she retorts.

"Um. Please sit down and stay quiet would sound better," suggests Grayson.

"They both mean the same thing."

"All good," I reply. "I'm not upset." But I am worried this might be necessary to prevent injury rather than due to Violet's impatience and drop my ass onto the dirt.

Violet draws runes on the drier parts of the earth—in white chalk and not blood. She joins me and Rowan in a circle on the ground, away from the memorial site, but close enough to see the edge of the trees. Grayson stays outside the circle, resting against a mossy trunk as he watches.

I've experienced Rowan and Violet's magic separately but not together. Earlier, Violet informed me that Rowan's magic will charge hers, which means only one person will shuffle through my memories. That's one too many for comfort.

Hell, yeah, I want to remember that evening, but I've thoughts about Violet that I no way want her to see. She's clueless about body language and subtle—or not so subtle—looks, but a window into my mind offers her everything. How will Violet react if she comes across the thoughts I have about her that I'd never say out loud to the girl?

Oh, man. No girl should have free rein inside a guy's head.

"Look at this as an opportunity to hold Violet's hand," says Rowan with a sly smile.

She shoots him a look and I sigh. Violet hovers an outstretched hand above each of our knees, as if ready to snatch them away at any moment. The three of us are already linked by circumstance, our lives wrapped up more than Violet would like, and my nerves settle because these people can help me. Perhaps Violet's motivations aren't as selfish as before. I smile to myself—perhaps a little more 'benevolent'.

As I take hold, Violet's soft skin couldn't be more opposite to her hard shell, and I'm distracted by how small and delicate her hand is in mine that's almost twice the size of hers.

Violet purses her lips as she stares at where our fingers join. "You've the same energy as Zeke."

Oh, great. I remind Violet of her dad. Not quite what I'm looking for. "Will I remember what you see, too?"

"Possibly. If not at the time, you will later because the magic will free the memories."

"Let's hope they're memories I'd actually like."

Rowan hasn't spoken to me much since earlier and when I asked if he's okay, he replied that he's thinking things through after last night. Whatever that means. I'm surprised he wasn't hauled in and asked questions. Why didn't Sawyer involve authorities?

As Violet takes Rowan's hand, she also takes a sharp breath and the two exchange a look that I struggle to comprehend. How does the bond feel? I'm aware non-bonded witches assist each other with magic in this way, but theirs must exist on a deeper level. There's a subtle difference

—they look at each other longer than Violet's usual nanosecond and even if she's closed off, there's a stillness about Rowan at odds with how he usually is around her. Has something happened between them?

I'll ask him.

I complete the circle as I close my fingers around Rowan's, and the force from the intense energy hits my mind sudden and hard, and the trees around lurch. Violet briefly squeezes my fingers tighter, a silent 'okay'.

"Do you often hold someone's hand and dig into their minds?" I ask cautiously. "You never touched me last time."

"No. You're the first. Shush."

I splutter. "Not dangerous at all, then?"

"Don't stress, Leif. If you die, Violet will use her other magic," says Grayson from where he stands behind.

"Not funny, dude," I snap, then look to Violet as the spell stirs around my head like I've drunk too much alcohol. "What if you break my mind?"

"I doubt that'll happen," she says. "And shush."

"'No' would've been a more reassuring answer, Vio— Fuck!" I almost tear my hand from Rowan's to hold against my head as the tearing sensation in my brain matches skin breaking from times I've had claws in chest.

Ears ringing and vision blurring, I attempt to stay upright. Nausea rises to join the pain, and with it an instinctive desire to slap away Violet's mental fingers. I clench my jaw against the scraping.

"It bloody hurts," I rasp out as the sensation worsens. "Like you're peeling skin off my body but in my brain."

Violet doesn't respond and continues to grip, eyes closed as she murmurs to herself. A spell? I flick a look at Rowan who's fixated on her, mouth thin with concern when he glances at me.

"That'll be the barrier," he says. "The magic is hard to get through because the spell doesn't want the defense pulling it off."

"Nice." I suck in a huge breath as another agonizing rip slashes at my mind. I can't do this.

But I have to.

Violet swears and pauses, the assault pausing as her mind wanders around the edge of mine.

Crap. You know when someone tells you not to think about something and you immediately do? I've just done that to myself.

Violet has a direct view of imagining kissing her outside that day. All the times I've stared at her ass, her breasts, every single unclean thought I've had about this girl presented like a personal movie to her.

Fuck. I squeeze my eyes as tight shut as I can, trying to wipe away those thoughts, and Violet jumps away too. What happened to only seeing memories from that night?

Uh. Like that one.

Oh. My. Fucking. God. I'll never look this girl in the eye again now she's seen that. Jesus, I hope Rowan's honest and isn't in my head too. This time I do begin to pull away, but Violet's nails dig into my hand. "Educational but irrelevant," she says.

Educational? The sudden hit of surprise snaps me out of the need to pull away, but the pain whipping through my mind stings and burns with pain I've never experienced or ever want to again. I yell out, vision blackening as an intense burn screams across every inch, like fire licking at my skin.

"Hold on, Leif, please," she urges. "I'm there."

Taking short breaths, I dim my awareness, retreating into the part of my mind where I hide when I'm threatened. Whatever Grayson went through, I understand on a small level because when shifters get a hold of me, it isn't ever pleasant.

Violet's voice echoes as if I'm submerged in water,

Rowan's too, and the pain turns to numbness like the burnt nerves have severed. I can't see or hear anything, barely aware of the touch.

Lost in a black hole, I'm unaware the pair no longer hold my hands until stones press into my cheek. I force my heavy eyes open and meet Rowan's grave ones as he holds out a hand to pull me up.

Unsteadily, I sit, immediately looking around for Violet as I support myself with a hand on the ground. If I weren't so weak I'd reach out and take hold of her. She's deathly pale and her nose bloodied, which she's wiping away in annoyance.

I can't ask as I push hair from my clammy face. Their 'vibe'? Bad.

"Please, no," I manage to whisper out. "Did I kill him?"

"Rory killed Wesley," says Violet flatly.

Should I sink with relief I didn't murder someone or share her new worry—whoever broke into Violet's room and drew the arrow knows.

"But he wasn't alone," she continues calmly.

"My uncle?" asks Grayson.

"Two male witches. A vamp couldn't create that spell in Leif's mind. Rory attacked you too, Leif, but they called him off you as if he was a dog." Violet moistens her lips. "This happened before."

"Rory attacked someone else?" I ask in horror.

She shakes her head. "No. Years ago. One incident that sliced through the accords between witches and shifters was Dominion witches using shifters to kill other shifters." Violet bites her lip. A trembling lip, totally unlike her.

"Mind controlled?" asks Rowan.

"No. Reanimated shifters."

"What the fuck? Rory was…" I swallow as she nods.

"At least one of the witches is a necromancer," says Violet.

"How?" I ask hoarsely

"Me and Eloise aren't the only ones out there. The magic isn't unique to the Thornbrook family line." Violet remains stiff and distant, and her aura disturbs me.

She's disturbed.

"Fuck," says Grayson as he sits beside Violet. He stares at the blood on her face and hands, then shuffles towards me instead.

"This changes everything. Someone is trying to frame me in order to attack Dorian, but the whole situation is bigger than that." She scrubs hard at her stained cheek with a sleeve. "I think the Dominion are back."

Chapter Twenty-Eight

VIOLET

I GRIP A HANDFUL OF THE SPARSE GRASS THAT GROWS IN THE clearing, as the truth triggers something I've never experienced.

Fear.

Rowan and Leif have less understanding than Grayson and I do about the old world, as their families weren't major players. The Petrescus and the Blackwood witches—who also created Dorian—were center stage in the conflict. The other main players from that part of history died or disappeared once our world imploded.

Grayson understands because his pulse picked up, yet he's stiller.

Even if this threat isn't the old Dominion organization, they've the same aim as their predecessors if they're committing atrocities: overthrow those in charge of our society using chaos from distrust.

My fear Rowan might cause trouble if he became uncontrolled now pales as much as he is right now. Leif looks the worse—I'm looking at the guy I saw injured in the woods that night, barely able to stay upright as Rowan and Grayson help move him to rest against a nearby trunk.

"You definitely need to speak to Dorian," says Rowan as I stand, woozy from the amount of energy I expended on that spell.

"Dorian will lose his shit," says Grayson.

"Probably what they want." Leif drags a shaking hand through his hair.

My changing world just slipped further from my grasp. "Grayson's worries earlier are correct. If I mention Petrescu as well as witches, Dorian will go straight for Grayson's uncle without stopping to think."

"And Grayson," replies Rowan.

Grayson's expression betrays nothing as he looks at me. What if Dorian's knee-jerk reaction causes more issues? "Rowan's right. We need more evidence before telling him."

Leif's eyes widen. "Not if we're dealing with the people you described!"

"Better than a psychotic Dorian 'dealing with' them." I wipe a hand over my forehead. "Honestly, you don't understand what Dorian hides beneath his facade."

"And if they're threatening his little girl…" says Rowan.

"I'm not his little girl," I say through clenched teeth.

"But you are, Violet. Look how he protected you for years —barely let you out of sight," says Grayson. "All of your family did."

"They didn't trap me. I didn't want to be part of the world and had no desire to leave my home."

"Which is weird," presses Grayson.

"I'm weird," I retort. "Life was simpler on the estate. Everything in its place. An unbroken routine. No people to interfere with my life."

"But you weren't 'living'," adds Rowan. "Look how shut down you were when you arrived at Thornwood."

"Don't bad mouth my parents," I growl. "My childhood didn't make me like this. I *am* this."

"Guys," says Leif with a sigh. "This won't help. Can we just agree that Violet isn't normal and never will be?"

"Thank you. At least you don't expect more of me."

He smiles. "I can't imagine you as anything different or would like you to be."

"Smooth, Leif," says Rowan beneath his breath.

Ah yes. Leif's accidental memories. Good grief. I'm glad I couldn't see much, but that does change matters between us. Why do these guys have to make my head hurt in this way?

"Also, we wouldn't have time to tell him today. There's Rory's wake this afternoon," I say.

"Violet," Rowan warns.

"How can we *not* go now? There's a chance that other shifters are dead or under influence. These witches might live nearby, or be at the wake," I say.

"And someone else might die," adds Grayson.

"Yes. That too," I add. "Nobody needs to see us, Rowan. Do you know where Kai's meeting his friends? Did he tell you last night?"

Rowan sucks his lips together rather than reply.

"Dude, you may as well tell Violet because you've no chance of stopping her," says Grayson. "Better she knows than wanders around in plain sight looking for the guy on her own."

"A lodge," mutters Rowan. "By the lake on Sawyer's land."

"Do you know exactly where this lodge is?" I ask, but Grayson already whipped out his phone. "Close to the shifter community?"

"Close enough," says Grayson as he scrolls through his phone. "Opposite bank to the shifters."

"Kai didn't go into detail, but I reckon he intends to

disrupt things like Viggo disrupted Wes's funeral," says Rowan.

"We can watch the lodge, and if Kai leaves for the wake, we can call authorities and watch and act if we need," says Grayson.

"And Leif?" asks Rowan. "He can't go."

"I'd rather he did," I reply and Rowan gawks at me. "We should stick together, especially if someone at Thornwood may be involved. Leif shouldn't go back to campus alone."

"I can look after myself," he grumbles.

"And what if 'whoever' more than wipes your memories this time, Leif? These people didn't kill you last time, but next time…? Especially if they discover Violet knows something," says Grayson. "Because they *will* discover."

I'm glad for Grayson's support, but Rowan's face remains grim. "You've got the pendant and powerful supes with you, Leif. I don't want anybody to hurt you."

Leif's eyes soften. "Yeah?"

"Yes." I tap the side of my head. "You have evidence in here." Rowan clears his throat and I glance at him. What? "Oh. And I wouldn't want you to die, Leif." A raised brow from Rowan. "Because that would be unpleasant and, unfortunately, you're not immortal."

"I think what Violet *means* is you're a nice guy and don't deserve to get hurt," says Rowan.

"Yes. That."

Why are the three laughing at me?

Still, Leif doesn't give me an answer.

"I'll go with you, but only if you speak to Dorian," says Rowan stiffly.

"What? And have him crash a shifter wake?"

"Uh. Isn't that what you're doing?"

"I won't get close—just watch Kai." Rowan's scoff gets my hackles up.

"Go to him straight after."

"I can't start a war," I reply.

"That's a bit overdramatic," says Leif.

I turn my eyes to his. "Again, you don't understand what Dorian is capable of and how triggered he'll be. And I think Eloise would tell him if I confided in her. He will literally strike with no evidence. And then what happens? Chaos."

"I'll go with you, Violet," says Grayson. "Whoever killed Rory might be another influenced shifter, or if not, there could still be another shifter murder. But I agree that you need to tell Dorian."

Huh. Well, if Rowan and Grayson agree on something, that's a start for *their* relationship, even if it's something I don't like.

"Leif, would you feel safer if you went back to Marlene?" asks Rowan. "If the shifters are occupied, they won't be interested in you."

"Way to sound like Violet," says Leif. "Must be rubbing off on you."

"The woman you stayed with—Marlene—is she in touch with Zeke or Ethan?" I ask.

He shakes his head. "No. She isn't officially involved with anything; Marlene's an old friend of Mom and Dad."

"And a shifter?" He nods. "Who does she work with?"

Leif chews his lip. "Marlene doesn't tell me who the shifters are since they'd face trouble if elders discovered some were going against them."

"Zeke or Ethan need to speak to these elders—they'll be more levelheaded about this," I say.

Rowan's shoulders relax—slightly. "Today?"

"I'll try to contact them, but I'm not mentioning anything about Leif's memories. Go with Leif to Marlene's, Rowan." His mouth opens. "I know, protective bonded witch who should be with me, but that's the point. Your response to danger could cause a problem."

"*Bonded?*" interrupts Grayson. "Holy fuck. Really?"

"Yes." I'm dismissive but Grayson stares at Rowan, who returns his look and says nothing. "And so, I'd rather keep us apart in case that interferes with our common sense."

"Like attending the wake isn't interfering already?" mumbles Rowan.

"Violet's right," says Leif. "We can't have you losing your shit if Violet's threatened."

"But—"

"But I'm fine with Grayson." I blow air into my cheeks. "In fact, I'm fine on my own, but Grayson offered."

Rowan's jaw hardens. "Call us if Kai heads to the wake. I don't want Violet anywhere near it without me."

"But—"

This time I'm the one interrupted. "That's called a compromise, Violet." Grayson smiles. "An unusual concept for you, but one that might help you learn in life."

And so starts the confusion. "Simple question: am I looking for Kai alone or with Grayson?"

Chapter Twenty-Nine

GRAYSON

WHO KNEW THAT SHARING MAJOR TRAUMA WITH Thornwood's weirdest and most suspicious witch would gain me entry to Violet's detective agency? Or should I say, Violet's collection of guys—typical witch, even though she isn't. Oh man, who knows what she is apart from the girl who consumes me as much as I'm desperate to consume her.

But I guess I'll hold back on that until I figure out whether Violet's desires remain for my blood only. I want more than that.

I'm not dumb, the group don't a hundred percent trust me yet and who could blame them? My track record isn't great and my family connections less so. Keep your friends close and your enemies closer—I'm still at the lower end of that scale, but at least they *believe* me. But I'll need to watch my behavior around Violet and her protective bonded witch who has a reputation for painful magic attacks.

World watch out if Violet accepts this bond more than she appears to—the pair would be lethal together.

We only know that the memorial is this afternoon and not the precise time or location. Will Kai still attend once Sawyer gets hold of him? Let's hope he arrives with his buddies at the lodge.

Rowan suggested that we don't return to the academy in case we've more trouble to face there and I make my way across town towards Sawyer's land with Violet as Leif heads away with Rowan.

As two vamps, we can move at a decent speed without them, although I reckon Leif could keep up even if Rowan couldn't. We reach the outskirts of the small community near the lake and then walk to the opposite side, where the lodge is located. As a vamp, I also hate large bodies of water and Violet isn't keen, but we need to wait close enough to the lodge to at least hear what happens if Kai arrives. On this side of the lake, shifters are less likely to scent us than if we were trawling around in case Kai decided to move closer to their settlement.

Satellite images of Sawyer's land picked out unmarked tracks and buildings—as well as the lodge, and other buildings a similar size are dotted around within cleared areas. This guy owns a lot of land. From the town border, across the lake his property encompasses, and to the village-like settlement belonging to the shifters. Much of the area is wooded, although he cleared around his imposing home and added stretches of lawns.

Me and Violet carefully approach the cedar lodge bordered by pine trees, which allows privacy for any who stay here and offers cover for snooping vamps. No voices or tire tracks. A large verandah wraps around the house, edged all around by a tall picket fence with Fleur de Lys shaped posts.

Fishing rods hang above a wood pile and seats made from wood to match the lodge allow visitors to enjoy the view. Have they positioned the building here to watch across the lake because the place has a great vantage point for the opposite bank?

To the left and behind the lodge, a metal shed with an open door houses a small motorboat, explaining the wooden jetty jutting into the river. At least the boat will be spotted if Kai chooses that means to crash the wake, since the trip across would take several minutes.

"I never realized the Sawyers owned this much land," I say as we pass the cedarwood building to find a less obvious spot to wait. "And how large the shifter settlement is. No wonder the elders are pissed that the Sawyers took their land."

"Yes. Perhaps if the shifters accepted my fathers' help rather than be bloody-minded, he could've intervened." Violet pauses and looks across the still lake.

"They'll need his help now," I reply, and we continue to tread the dirt and into the trees behind the lodge.

"Maybe the elders will finally listen to one of my fathers."

We come across a clearing close by where a couple of fallen logs create makeshift benches. As Violet sits on the moss-covered seat, I scuff the center of the area with my boot, where the ground's blackened. Remains of a fire? At least a smaller one than the kids usually have for their 'gatherings' on the edge of town.

Beer cans in the nearby bushes? I'm guessing Kai and his mates.

"I'll ask Ethan to contact me," Violet says and looks at her phone. "Although I'll probably send him into full panic—I've only called Ethan once, and that was to give him my number."

"Where is he? Far?" I ask and sit on the makeshift seat opposite her. I've never seen or met either Zeke or Ethan, but heard they're more approachable than Dorian, even though many are equally scared of the shifter hybrids.

"Ethan's too far away to reach me today. I'll just mention

I've an acquaintance who wants to speak with him." I chuckle at her. "What?"

"So, you won't tell him about the beginnings of a town war between shifters and humans."

"No. That won't be sensible. What a silly suggestion, Grayson." I shake my head. Always the literal with her. "I have to respect Leif's wishes and wait. He has Rowan and the pendant; Leif will be safe in the meantime."

"And you have me," I reply.

"Yes. But I don't need you."

She doesn't look up from the phone as I clutch my chest. "You're a heartbreaker, Violet," I tease.

"My unfortunate desire for your blood doesn't automatically create an emotional closeness, Grayson," she says flatly.

Still, Violet doesn't look at me. No closeness *yet*. "Like Rowan and the bond doesn't bring you closer?" *Oh, so quiet, Violet.* She's either ignored me or I've hit on something. "Or not? Are you closer to him than me or Leif now?"

"I don't have time for this."

"Look at me." She pulls a face and our gazes lock. "We have plenty of time."

"I'm busy trying to figure things out." Violet tenses as I stand. "What are you doing?"

"Sitting next to you to read your notes."

And because I'm craving that closeness as much as your blood. Violet watches me warily and I smile. If she protests, Violet will admit more than she likes. Is now a good time to broach what happened last night?

The twin responses of desire and fear overcame me when Violet morphed into that savage creature focused on her blood lust. The same lust took control of me many times in the past and there was a thrill last night that I could share this with someone as strong as me. A thrill I decided to keep in check. When the time is right, I'll know.

"Violet, about last—"

"When will you next see your uncle?" she asks casually, halting me.

"I'm supposed to meet him in a couple of days."

She gazes at me, blue eyes as glacial as she often is. "I'd like to meet him."

"Uh. No?"

"Oh. Not straightaway, but I will ensure one day I do. I saw the color Rowan lost and felt his horror after he looked into your mind—when the time is right, I'd like Dorian to deal with him." She runs her tongue along her top teeth. "As I told Leif, I'm intolerant of bullies, as is my father."

"Intolerant." I snort a laugh. "But, yeah, I want to deal with him too. Alone, without his bastard friends."

"You might need assistance based on your weakness against them." My eyes go wide at her unintended insult, but she returns to scrolling on her phone. "We need to take turns in watching the lodge for Kai's arrival."

"And if he doesn't appear, how long do we wait until heading to the shifters? When and where are their rites likely to take place?"

"While I was upstairs at the party, Rowan spoke to Kai, and he said lakeside, so somewhere along the bank. No idea what time though."

"How convenient Kai chose somewhere out of reach, but where he could boat across and reach them." Violet nods. "I hope Leif can persuade Marlene to help further. She can speak to the shifters who help and ask them to meet us. Someone in their community needs to know about the necromancy. More could be in that… state."

"I'm confident Ethan can arrange a meeting."

I tap the toes of my boots together as Violet lapses back into her investigative world. "Why didn't others know what Rory was?"

"Because there wouldn't be signs, since even *he* didn't

know." Violet clicks her phone off. "Constructs are under the witch's control, but they keep all their memories and are unaware. Apart from reanimated witches—things are hit and miss with them."

"Hit and miss?"

"Sometimes a witch's magic resists the necromancer's spell, or other witches' minds become totally messed up when touched by that darkness. Some witches forget who they are entirely."

"Right. So, if Rowan died, you'd need to turn him, not use necromancy."

Violet, as usual, misses my joke completely. "Rowan will not die. Don't be ridiculous."

She said it herself though—the guy isn't immortal. He will die one day. But I nod. "What if Viggo is one of these 'things'?"

"I don't know. If I'd looked into his or Rory's head when we fought at the memorial, I would've known."

"They're mindless enough," I say with a smile.

"Oh. Their minds wouldn't be blank, but a void. Totally black. I'm irritated with myself for not doing so, but I wasn't looking for the possibility at the time. If I can get close enough to any other shifters and into their heads, I'll know. That's why we need Ethan's help to get nearer to them."

A void? Life as someone's creature would be bad enough, but a literal living death... I shudder.

The nearby rumble of a car engine interrupts us, as we both pause at once, again hearing from a greater distance. Whoever this is approaches the area, driving along the track through the woods that leads to the lodge.

"That has to be Kai and his minions," says Violet.

"We're far enough away that they won't see us," I reply. Our spot here is a few minutes' walk for humans, definitely enough for vamps to hear if they approach.

Violet stands and brushes the dirt from her ass, distracting me from her insane suggestion. "No. We get closer."

"Only close enough to hear more clearly," I warn her. "The last thing we need is a confrontation—I doubt Kai's happy about last night."

"Yes. But we can also watch what Kai does and where he goes—and intervene if necessary."

Intervene 'Violet-style'?

She slants her head as we wait for the engine to cut off, then hear male voices. Three. Violet nods at me and we make our way towards a partially hidden vantage point where the trees thin and allow us a closer look.

The driver parked the expensive SUV at the edge of the dirt track and close to the shed, so only the shiny silver hood is visible. The door to the lodge is now open and whoever walked inside no longer speaks. Violet makes to edge out of the trees, and I grab her baggy cardigan sleeve. Scowling at me, she slaps at my hand and I'm *this close* to taking hold of that hand.

Creeping forward, so lightly that nothing underfoot makes a sound, Violet emerges from the hiding area and moves nearer. Sure, she's away from the front verandah, but Violet's in the open.

The silver SUV is a Range Rover with a SAWYER2 license plate. Either daddy buys Kai expensive shiny toys or Sawyer's one of the people in the house. Violet's eyes narrow.

I sneak after her to pick up the scent.

Human.

"Sawyer or Kai and buddies?" I whisper.

"Witch."

Huh? "In there?"

"Can't you detect the magic?" She purses her lips and edges forward, so I grab her sleeve again.

"The witch might detect you, Violet."

"Witches aren't as keen sensed as us. Let me go. I'm not

stupid enough to march inside the lodge." She yanks herself away from me.

"I don't want to go fucking fishing," comes Kai's pissed voice.

"I am not leaving you alone today." I glance at Violet as Sawyer replies. Where is Kai's gang? "I do not want more trouble, and certainly not your involvement if there is."

Something scrapes along a wooden floor. "You don't usually care what I do."

Then I *do* sense the witch—a male voice I don't recognize. "Listen to your father." He's softly spoken, an accent similar to Rowan's. Related to him? Possibly, but all upper class witches sound the same to me. "Stay here, Kai."

"And who are you to tell me what the fuck to do?" Kai retorts. "Who is this?"

"Someone to help protect you," Sawyer replies.

Kai scoffs. "Yeah? The guy might need a few more muscles against a shifter." He pauses. "Or is he another vamp? Doesn't look like one."

"No, I am not," the witch says tersely. "But I do have skills that help your father."

"A witch? Since *when* do you trust witches?" asks Kai. "You won't let them in the house."

"I'm making new connections, Kai. Maxwell aids me with business, that's all. I thought he'd enjoy an afternoon fishing with us."

Violet laughs beneath her breath. "Is Kai stupid?"

"Why do you think the witch is here?" I whisper.

"You saw how Sawyer behaved earlier. He wants Kai out of danger." She purses her lips. "I'd deduce that the witch is taking over our assumed role in keeping Kai safe, but after looking at Leif's memories, I doubt that's the reason for the witch's presence. This could be one of those I saw."

Chapter Thirty

GRAYSON

"Do you know the name Maxwell?" Violet shakes her head. "Send Rowan a message. Ask if he does."

As Violet types, I survey our surroundings. If the three plan to fish, will they choose the jetty or boat? We need to back off in case they leave the lodge, because we'd be in full view if they sit on the jetty.

Footsteps on wood outside. Verandah. "Violet," I whisper. "Come away."

"Can you guarantee his safety?" asks Sawyer as a door closes, the entrance still out of sight.

"Have I ever let you down, Christopher?" replies Maxwell.

"Why not just make Kai another pendant?"

"Isn't keeping Kai here a better idea than letting him loose on a day like today?" He pauses. "Tell your brat son to behave."

"And the shifters won't come for him?" asks Sawyer.

"The one who works for me won't want to leave the wake,

so if I call him, his absence will be suspicious." As the pair talk, there's pissed stomping around inside of the lodge.

"A shifter is working with a witch?" I ask incredulously.

"I don't believe the witch meant call the shifter on the phone." Violet's eyes turn to me. "There's at least one other, Grayson."

"Witch?"

"No. Shifter construct—reanimated and under a witch's control. That's what Maxwell means. No way would Sawyer know about that either."

"How do *you* know?"

Violet waves a hand. "I don't and hope I'm wrong."

"Yeah, this shifter could simply be a traitor."

"Hmm." Violet flicks her tongue against her teeth. "I'd rather fear the worst. Less chance of disappointment. Plus, I'd like to see who this necromancer is."

"Why?"

"To ask for lessons." My mouth drops open. "Good grief, Grayson. I wasn't serious."

"Yeah, well, sarcasm doesn't normally come from you, and could you please choose your moments?"

She sighs. "Do you people want me to attempt to emulate your kind or not? Now be quiet. I'm missing their conversation." I blink at her as she tips her head again. "We need to identify this witch."

"I hope Sawyer sticks around. What if the witch wants a new victim?"

"Yes. I had considered that," she says, eyes ahead.

"I want to see he's safe before we leave," says Sawyer, and I refocus on him.

"Kai won't get past my magic, and neither will a shifter. Exactly like your home. Now, please, stop questioning me."

Sawyer doesn't reply and I can imagine how pissed *he'll* be that someone's speaking down to him.

"Oh. Smart." Violet edges backwards towards the tree line. "The witch plans to 'secure' Kai here."

"Huh. I bet you'll hear Kai yelling at them to let him out from all the way across the lake."

"I very much doubt a human could shout that loudly, Grayson."

"No, I meant… Never mind."

"A shame for him that Sawyer is as stupid as his son." Violet looks down as her phone sounds. "A witch who reanimates people and encourages murder isn't likely to be a human ally. Now, if he's connected to Wesley's death, that begs the question: why?"

"I've thought about this. Maybe Wes's murder was a mistake?" I suggest. "And that's why the witch killed his construct?"

Violet's eyes widen. "Oh. Rory killed the wrong human."

"Oh, fuck. Was Kai the intended victim?" I swipe a hand down my face.

"What if the necromancer told Rory to kill the human who upset Viggo, expecting Kai and him to fight. Apart from me, Viggo also had 'exchanges' with Wes *and* Kai." Violet holds her head. "Or his target was Kai specifically, and they look similar in the dark?"

"A possibility. If the witches orchestrated Kai's failed murder, we can't leave the area today. Not until I've tried to release Kai from the lodge. And if the magic trumps mine, we'll stay in case the witches correct their mistake." I nod at her phone. "What did Rowan say?"

"He doesn't know the name—wants a description. That's our next task." I'm stunned for a moment as she steps even more in possible view, but I manage to grab her before she gets far. "Will you cease taking hold of my clothes, Grayson? I need a photo of this man for Rowan."

"Fuck, Violet. You're not an undercover detective…" I trail off. "Not a professional one."

"Yet."

I laugh, and she gives me her best scowl. "You want to be a detective?"

"I'm rather enjoying solving the puzzle—especially a difficult one that frustrates me."

"Puzzle? *Murders*, Violet. You want to help people?" I ask incredulously.

"That's a side effect of my actions. No, I like using my extensive intelligence on interesting things." She pauses. "Stop distracting me. Part of my newly adopted role involves preventing more crimes occurring. Such as another death."

"Have you lost your mind?" I gawk at her. "What happened to the girl who wanted nothing to do with anybody —human, witch, or vampire?"

Violet pauses and turns. "I'm still selective about who I acquaint myself with and care little for those I've no reason to interact with. No individual is superior to me nor will achieve such status. *That* is my motivation. The murderer will *not* escape me."

She spins back around, phone in hand, and I moisten my lips as I stare at the petite girl. Violet's obsession with these crimes has no root in good deeds, nor even in proving she didn't murder anybody.

Violet just wants to outsmart everybody.

Chapter Thirty-One

GRAYSON

Sawyer returns inside to speak to his loud, angry son again, while the witch guy stands on the pebbled bank, looking over the calm lake. The guy's about my height, slim figure, with a padded black jacket and brown hair swept up in a modern style. We can't see any more as he faces away, talking on the phone. Frustratingly, one-sided conversations are hard to figure out, especially as most of Maxwell's responses are 'yes' or 'no'.

Violet's figure blurs from beside me to behind a broader trunk, closer to the lodge. *Crap, Violet.* As Maxwell continues to face the water and not our direction, Violet can't get a clear image of him from our vantage point, and I'm silently pleading her not to approach the witch.

Predicting Violet's behavior? Impossible.

Sawyer reappears and calls to Maxwell. The witch turns around to face the lodge, but his back to us, before wandering slowly away from where we watch, and around the perimeter. Next, Kai reappears and storms towards the

SUV. How much danger is he in? I like the guy, or as much as I like any human—he's never done wrong by me—and he shouldn't suffer for whatever shit his dad got himself mixed up in.

"Take the tackle inside and sort what we need," says Sawyer as Kai retrieves a large box. "Pack up some beers too. You'll find a case in the fridge," he adds as Kai passes, the sour-faced kid not looking at him.

Kai stomps up the steps, the witch still not in sight, and Sawyer remains outside, hands dug in his pockets. The witch's shoes crunch on pebbles as he continues his circuit of the lodge and moves closer to us. I firmly grab Violet's arm to drag her backwards before he sees anything. She swears at me and drops the phone, her furious eyes wider as I clamp a hand over her shout of protest.

In the corner of my vision, the witch pauses and lifts his head, on alert.

"Fuck," I mutter and pull the protesting Violet backwards. If she's about to yell at me, I'm pulling Violet further out of here, so I drag her through the woods until we're well out of sight and hearing. Interestingly, she doesn't bite my hand this time.

Although I do get a magical hit that blinds me and my arms slacken, muscles becoming jelly as I drop my hold.

"Do not interfere," she snaps, her eyes now furious black. "I can move as fast as you and was about to. Why would I risk him seeing me?"

"I panicked," I mutter and massage my aching temples.

"I told you to stop grabbing me. I don't need this distraction, Grayson," she says as she shoves me in the chest, breathing like a human who ran twice as far as I pulled her.

And there it is—her visceral response to my blood, clouding her energy and pushing her own blood close to the surface. The desire to take and be taken.

Did my touching Violet trigger her *that* easily? Again,

interesting. Inhaling deeply, Violet turns her back. "Do not place a single finger on me again, Grayson."

"I said, I panicked." Walking up behind Violet, I pause at her shoulder. Her natural scent joins that from the blood and my fingers itch to move her glossy hair to one side and place my lips on her neck. Not to bite and satisfy myself with Violet's blood, but to taste the sweetness on her skin.

Violet thinks I only want her blood? She's so much more than that.

"*If* you do what I can *clearly* see in your mind, Grayson, I will pin you to that tree behind me with paralyzing magic, and you won't move until I say you can."

Her voice is infused with violent promise, but I can't help myself. "Sounds fun."

Violet whirls around, and I drop the amusement as she seizes me around the throat, gripping hard enough to partially choke me. "Like this is fun?"

Whoa.

Her teeth bare. "I am not here to for a bloodthirsty tryst, Grayson Petrescu. I do not appreciate your triggering behavior, and neither will *you* if you push me to the state I was in last night. Especially if this idiocy interferes with our purpose for being here this afternoon."

In that moment, I see her father. I've never met Dorian but heard the stories—how he snaps in a heartbeat when something upsets him, even minor. An accidental threat to Violet's self-control? I should've pulled back, not teased her, because fury pumps Violet's blood harder, the scent maddening.

"Fuck, Violet," I choke out. "Let go."

She tiptoes until our faces are closer, and her fast breaths touch my lips. "You guys treat me like a girl whose struggles to deal with the world are endearing. You all want to care for the pretty little thing who looks so delicate." My eyes widen as the pressure on my throat intensifies. "I am not delicate. I am not endearing. And neither is this dark thing that lives inside me."

"Yeah, and you overreact." I snatch her wrist and pull, Violet's nails scratching as her fingers drag across my neck. "A lot and often."

Our gazes lock. However much she shows me what lies beneath, Violet will never frighten me because I've looked into dark, determined, and disturbed eyes many times. My own. Nothing else is spoken as our twin heartbeats synchronize, something I'm sure disturbs Violet as much as our effect on each other. Her eyes move to where she scratched my throat.

"You're fortunate that didn't draw blood," she says casually. "Now, can we return to the reason we're here?" And just like that, Violet regains herself. She scoots off and returns with her phone seconds later, before zooming the image on the screen with two fingers. "I got a shot, but it's too blurry. I'll send to Rowan, anyway."

I'm stunned into silence and stillness, my skin feeling as if her fingers still press there. Although her action mimicked others who've held me by the throat, Violet hasn't scared me.

Quite the opposite.

Violet's words echo as I stare at the girl who's returned to her task—who walked away from me and from the girl she hides. One day, I'll meet that dark thing, and I'm counting the days until I do.

Chapter Thirty-Two

GRAYSON

THE SUV CONTAINING SAWYER AND MAXWELL MOVES AWAY from the lodge, the smooth running engine ensuring they leave as quietly as possible. Violet lapsed into silence after that crazy response to me, losing herself in the world of Violet Blackwood where her brain never stops collecting and processing. Does she think of others more since the changes the bond caused? Allow people into her mind the way she denied she does at the graveyard?

I suspect yes. The changes in her are subtle, but she isn't the girl from the graveyard that night.

"Was the witch warding the lodge when he walked around? I can't see any runes," I reply as we take the opportunity to get closer now the SUV left.

"Not all magic is visible, Grayson."

"I know. I merely asked a question," I snap back.

Ignoring me, or oblivious, she edges closer to the lodge, and I hold back. "How long before Kai tries to leave?"

"Not long if he's meeting his friends," I suggest.

"And why aren't they here?"

"Maybe the gang changed their plans after Sawyer told Kai *his* plans? Kai might call them now?"

Violet's lips purse. "Only if the witch was dumb enough to leave Kai with an operational phone."

"Hmm. And how long until he kicks off?"

"He won't be able to kick anything off. That magic will be strong."

"No. Kicks off—starts yelling. Do we let him know we're out here?" I ask.

Violet paces towards the back of the house and pauses to peer at the tire tracks in the dirt before wandering towards the open shed. She's in view of the window, which might make my question pointless if Kai sees her first.

"Violet!" I urge quietly.

She looks over her shoulder. "Why look at me in that way? Kai isn't likely to burst from the building and attack me in a useless fashion. I want to check if there's magic elsewhere in the area."

"And the magic surrounding the house?"

"Strong but well-cloaked. Most wouldn't sense it, including you as a vamp." She crosses her arms. "Hence, I'd like to search for *hidden* magic. I bet this isn't Maxwell's first visit to the lodge."

"*I* think we need to get Kai out of here," I say.

Violet flicks her tongue against her teeth. "I'd like to see if the witch returns, if he's alone, and what he intends."

I raise my eyes skyward. There's no possible way to get Violet away from here. "If we wait, I want Rowan and Leif here too."

"If they agree." She approaches the house and crouches close to where the witch paused earlier and runs fingertips along the ground. "A barrier without runes. Interesting."

"Yeah?" As I join her in crouching, I steady myself on the ground and swear as a screaming pain surges from my arm to my heart.

"Be careful, by the way," she says.

"Why didn't that hurt you?" I groan and massage the middle of my chest.

"It tickled."

"And you didn't tell me, why?" I ask.

Blue eyes turn to mine, a smile playing at her lips. "You never asked."

Like me and the pendant. Good thing she smiled. "If the magic hit *me* hard, what would happen to Kai? Would this kill him?"

"Kai won't be able to open the door. I expect this magic is designed to kill an intruder." She laughs. "Like *us*. Only an imbecile would think that'd work."

"Hmm. Well, Rowan and Leif are on their way." The atmosphere darkens as her eyes do again. "I contacted them earlier, after Maxwell and Sawyer left. Rowan needs to know we're waiting for the witch to return. Four's better than two."

"To get hurt?" she retorts and stands.

"Listen, Violet. You're not infallible yourself," I jump up to look down on her. "And we're a group. Our decision to stay apart no longer stands."

"Unless someone tears my heart out and burns me, I'm fine."

"*If* you're immortal. *Are* you?"

She blinks. "I had this conversation recently. I haven't died yet, so I don't know. Presumably I am, since my parents are and I'm part-vampire."

"Presumably. That's enough to satisfy Violet Blackwood?" I shake my head. "Sorry. But I'm keeping the risk as low as possible."

With one last black look and grumbling, she walks away.

Sure, a spell or attack wouldn't fully kill an immortal supe, but a serious injury to a non-immortal Violet could lead to a permanent death. That worries me.

I take in my surroundings and understand why humans want to visit the quiet lakeside location, away from the stench of traffic and odors spilling from fast food places in town, to the open space of water reflecting the clear sky. And people… no people. Only quiet birdsong.

Only quiet birdsong.

"Violet!" I cross to where she's poking at the ground with a stick. "Why is Kai not shouting?"

"Good question." A part-drawn rune disturbs the dirt around her, but Violet doesn't comment as she wanders back to the lodge. I tense, jaw clenching as she not-very-quietly walks up the stairs and onto the verandah, only flinching slightly as she passes through the magic.

"Kai?" she calls, pauses, then hammers a fist on the door. "Kai!"

"Nothing?" I ask. "Can you break the magic?"

"Not without finding the source." Drawing her leg back, she slams a boot into the door, a not so subtle reminder that she isn't a delicate girl as the wood splinters. "Kai?"

"Is he in there?"

"Where else would he go?" She scans the room. "The Sawyers do like their opulence and expense."

"And Kai?" I press.

"Do you think you can get through the barrier if you try hard enough?" she asks. "Or are you waiting there for Rowan and Leif? I can sense one human in here and nobody else."

"Just locate Kai and the source of the magic," I say. "I'll watch out for anybody coming."

I gaze up at the pitched roof where windows span the upper story beneath and where a balcony with plush cushioned chairs take advantage of the location. Can't Kai jump, or does the magic extend upwards? Mind you, there's a bigger drop than most humans could manage without injury.

Or doesn't Kai know that he's trapped?

The deceptive serenity outside remains, everything silent from within the house too, and Violet returns to the porch. "Found Kai. He's either asleep or drugged or under a spell. Hard to tell."

"Where?" I stride over and hop up the steps onto the verandah, forgetting about the spell until an electric-type shock smacks at each place my body touches the barrier. Holding my breath, like that'd make any difference, I shove my way through. I've experienced worse than this before.

Violet's correct about the expense, totally at odds with the rougher nature outside, even if they've attempted a rustic feel with a large stone fireplace and wooden floors. The leather sofa that Kai lies on, mouth open and bottle sliding from his hand definitely doesn't fit the image. The guy's in the maroon and white varsity jacket and jeans he walked inside wearing and could be a kid passed out after too many beers, face pale and drool at one corner of his mouth. I'm a breath away from backing out of the lodge—I've come across too many dead bodies recently and although I can't see blood, I'm wary about approaching.

"He spilled his beer, not blood on the floor. Not dead," says Violet casually.

My body still aches from stepping through the magic, like sunburn uncomfortably heating my skin, and I rub my stinging neck. "Must be magic. One beer wouldn't do that to him."

Then I sense them. Witch and shifter. Close, but they haven't reached the lodge yet. I moisten my lips and look at Violet, who shakes her head to my silent question.

Leif and Rowan?

No.

Fuck. "Is this the same witch?" I whisper.

"I'm unsure, but a shifter with a witch worries me." She glances down at Kai. "We get him upstairs. Lock and ward a room. There's only one reason a pair like that would come here."

"They're here to *kill* him?" I glance towards the window. No car. The approaching pair are still walking from the direction we did. Hidden.

Violet's comments about not being a little girl again hit home when I turn back to see her effortlessly dragging Kai over the woven brown rug towards a set of stairs leading upwards. Bruises might be the least of the injuries Kai's facing today, but I grab his legs and help so his ass doesn't bump as we head upstairs.

We dump Kai on the bed and Violet quietly closes the door and leans against it, sizing up the room. A king-sized bed, covered in plush cream linens, and plenty of colorful pillows faces the balcony, and a separate door beside a walk-in wardrobe must lead to a bathroom.

"Can we get out of here using blood runes?" I ask.

"*We* could, but not with Kai—he'd need to be conscious to take part in the spell, and if we leave him, our presence here will be pointless." She taps her lips and crouches by Kai, who now lies on his front. Still alive. Fortunately. "He's spelled. Look in the bathroom for something I can draw a rune with. Eye pencil, lipstick, whatever."

"To break the spell?"

"No. Protect Kai while we figure out what to do." She points at the balcony. "We take Kai and leave that way once the witch and shifter walk inside the lodge. There could be others, and I don't want to fight anyone if Kai's not protected."

Dutifully, I open and slam drawers in the grey tiled bathroom, finally finding a bag filled with make-up.

"Here." I throw the lipstick I locate to Violet, who moves

to the door and begins drawing in pink across the whole frame.

"I'm now happy that you asked Rowan and Leif to follow. How far are they?" Violet asks as she reaches the top of the frame with the lipstick.

"They're driving. A few minutes."

What the fuck do we do? Of course, we're capable of fighting off a single witch and shifter between us, but also protecting Kai? That's a problem.

I rub a hand across the back of my neck as the pair approach, one figure taller and bulkier than the other, and kneel on the carpet so I'm not visible through the expansive windows. "Will these wards work?"

"The ones around the house? Could be the same witch who can cancel the magic. Mine? Depends on how powerful the witch is," she says, face stern. "Rowan's magic is often stronger than mine, as he's powerful and I'm hybrid. This witch's might match Rowan, but the shifter won't be able to pass through unless my wards break."

"*You* should leave." I gesture at the balcony.

"No. Why?"

"If anything happens, I won't die. My uncle proved that."

Disdain covers Violet's face. "They won't get a chance to injure me badly. I'll tear them apart first."

Stairs creak and I exchange a glance with Violet. The potency of the second scent with the witch's adds a new layer of trouble—he's shifted, not in human form.

"What animal is he?" I whisper.

"Bear?" she suggests. "Viggo's gang is Ursa. And the Ursa cap that was left at Kai's memorial suggests a connection."

"Shit." I rub a hand across the top of my head. "What if we need to kill one of them to get us all out? Then there'll be a body!"

Violet takes another calculating glance around the room. "We'll risk it—take Kai over the balcony. I know we're too high for a human to jump, but he's unconscious. Put him over your shoulder."

"You said yourself—what if there're more witches or shifters around?" I urge. "No."

She takes a long, annoyed breath. "Fine. We don't kill the shifter."

"Or the witch?"

Violet shrugs.

Oh, man.

A male voice. An animal snuffling at the door. Maybe taking Kai and running would be a good idea? I push Violet behind me as something slams against the wood. Violet grumbles and pushes back at me to stand side by side. "Runes," she says. "He can kick the door down but won't cross."

"I bloody hope so," I mutter. Now they're inside the building, I walk over to pull open the balcony doors. If we fight, I'm not keen on hitting glass again for a good number of reasons. "Leave, Violet. I'll deal with this."

"Stop trying to be a hero," she snaps at me. "We do this together. Rowan and Leif won't be far; we hold these two off until they get here."

The smooth wooden door splinters in the center, interrupting my response. A bear lurches forward, paws raised, and slathering teeth bared, but the magic barrier stands, and he smacks into it then falls back. Shit, the thing's twice the size of me—at least. The powerful shoulders in the hulking brown creature flex as he readies himself to try again, yellow eyes with barely any pupils fixated on Kai.

"Wait," demands the witch beside him, and the bear, twice his size, sits like an obedient puppy.

"I enjoy being right but, in this case wish I was not," Violet says evenly as we both stare at the witch through the invisible magic.

This is Maxwell—he's wearing the same black jacket as

the witch we glimpsed, brown hair artfully swept upwards from his slim face. His thin lips spread into a smile.

"Hello, Violet Blackwood. How lovely to meet you," he says in his posh English accent, and places a hand on the animal's head. "I see you have your pet too."

I growl as he chuckles at me.

Chapter Thirty-Three

GRAYSON

"You can't get into the room, *Maxwell*," says Violet. "I suggest you leave before your day becomes miserable and painful."

"You'd let me walk away, knowing what I am?" he says, mock pouting. "Not capture me in your Blackwood mind-control and take me away for *punishment*?"

"What are you?" I ask.

"A witch," he says scornfully, then pats the panting bear on the head. "And this is my loyal companion."

"And are you a necromancer?" asks Violet calmly, but he replies with nothing but a steady gaze. "If you work with Sawyer, why are you threatening his son?"

My instincts spring to alert as a distinctive scent joins that of the two intruders—wood smoke. "Violet. He set a fire."

Maxwell smiles. "Neither of you would hang around in the vicinity of a fire—one of two things that can permanently kill your kind. Just leave Kai with us. My friend will take care of him."

The smoke triggers my deep-seated instinct to get the hell away before the heat draws any closer, but I grit my teeth. Am I right? Has this witch seriously set fire to a building he's standing in?

"Yes, I have Grayson." His smug smile grows. Of course, he's a bloody mind reader.

I'm ripped in two by my heartfelt need to stay in the thick of whatever happens next or saving myself, hating that my survival instinct tries to trample away the impulse to protect Violet. I don't care what she says, Violet can't face everything alone.

Rowan wouldn't walk away. Neither will I.

"I'll follow you off the balcony once my friend *attends* to Kai, and I draw a rune on him." Violet remains expressionless. "I really must practice more. Blackwood runes are *so* complex."

"Hmm. Did this shifter kill Wes and Rory? Who is he?" she asks and nonchalantly pulls out her phone. "Do give me more details."

"This one didn't kill Wesley."

"You'll need to be more specific," she says. "Do you mean this undead shifter only killed Rory? Did Rory make a mistake and kill the wrong human?"

The witch stares at Violet with barely hidden irritation. He'll learn Violet never reacts the way people would like—if he survives that long. "Why would I tell you?"

"Oh, you don't need to. We already figured this out; I just want confirmation." She doesn't look at him, typing on her screen. "Rory was your last 'pet', and he killed the wrong person, the mistake then leading to the end of his non-life. I merely require confirmation that Kai's the original victim, which you've now confirmed by your presence here. Just a couple more details if you'd be so kind. Who is this shifter and why do you want to kill Kai?" She looks up. "And who are *you*?"

"Shame your witch boy isn't here to strengthen your magic, little hybrid," he sneers. "Your runes are too weak."

I recoil as the witch takes a step into the room, and I toss a wild look at Violet as Maxwell crosses through her barrier. She closes her eyes and jerks her head, sending the witch backwards to slam against the wall in the hallway behind.

"I didn't invite you in. Answer the question. I asked more nicely than I usually would," she says calmly.

The bear lunges forward too and Violet hands out the same treatment, the bear thrown to the top of the stairs and denting the wall.

"And I am not weak." Violet's pupils grow, her irises losing the blue for black, a less-than subtle reminder what her other half is. "I'll demonstrate if you don't leave this building."

"But darling girl, I've broken your wards."

Ouch. That patronizing tone won't help what happens to him next.

Violet's changes start before I finish that thought—she isn't entirely vampiric in her hemia form, her face retains human features rather than twisting into the unnatural visage designed to strike horror in the victim. Still, her predatory and intimidating presence grows and my heart thumps for different reasons as I look at her.

Two of us. Two of them. Who takes on who?

The answer comes from the bear, who launches himself into the room, heading straight for Kai on the bed. With a snarl, Violet springs onto the creature's back and her elongated teeth rip into its neck, the sight of the girl a fraction of its size gripping on horrifyingly amusing.

"Don't kill him, Violet!" I call out, pausing to deal with Maxwell before I intervene.

Maxwell laughs. *Laughs.* I spin to him, changing, my hemia state fully visible, with none of Violet's subtleties. Ordinarily, I'd target him for his witch blood, but a greater desire overrides that—stop him. *Maxwell* murdered the guys:

he created the situation and helped frame Violet with the rune.

"Don't kill me." The witch's words aren't a plea, but a quiet warning. "How will Violet solve her little mystery if you kill a man with evidence? Don't you want to know who I work for?"

Smoke fills the stairwell behind, the lodge's wooden construction perversely giving the fire a cedar scent that humans choose to burn and enjoy. I blank out the instinct to run, waiting for my moment to attack the witch. But I can't. I'll lose control and kill him, and that'll land me in all kinds of shit.

No. Keep him *thinking* I will.

Maxwell holds his ground as I bring my teeth closer to his face and the twin snarling behind me continues—the bear's and Violet's.

"And if Violet kills a shifter?" Maxwell shakes his head and clicks his tongue, showing no fear. "The town would have the proof they need for all *three* murders."

"You already killed that shifter," I snarl, teeth and claws desperate to sink into the arrogant bastard. "Who is he? Or she?"

"End his life for a second time and you'll see." Maxwell mock gasps and places a hand over his mouth. "Oh, dear. Violet's halfway there already."

"Violet!" I turn to the struggle close to where Kai's motionless on the bed, blood running from a gash in the bear's neck, both of them covered in bleeding scratches. "Don't kill him!"

"But if she lets go of my pet, he'll kill Kai," muses Maxwell. "Who'll then die in a fire, in a strange mirror of what almost happened to Wesley."

"You fucking bastard!" I yell and lurch at him. "I'll fucking kill *you* and free the shifter."

"Is that what you think will happen?" He steps back, throwing out a spell, and I take the hit as it slugs me in the chest, ready to tear his smug face off.

But Violet's frenzy... I look desperately between her and the witch. Which do I stop?

"Or maybe Violet could kill her Petrescu enemy?" suggests the witch. "That *really* would upset the council. What if people decided Dorian sent her to Thornwood for that exact reason?"

No. Time. For. This. Bullshit. "Violet!" I yell again. "Get control. Please."

As I look in shock at the bizarre scene of a bloodied girl wrestling a bear, a slicing pain rips along my arm, and I whip my head round. The witch stands with a large kitchen knife in his hand, smirking at the slashed wound as he grips the black handle.

"Hey, at least if she attacks you, Violet won't kill the shifter," mocks Maxwell.

I whirl around. *Get Violet out. Kill the witch. Take Kai.*

Fucking *run*.

I throw myself at Violet and the bear, where she clings on with her teeth and clawed nails as he thrashes. Her head snaps around, lips drawn back as she scents me. I tear her from the animal, Violet's nails ripping through the shifter's skin as I toss her as far as I can from me and the creature. She falls heavily onto her backside on the balcony and gives a guttural yell.

This bloodied hybrid looks like a fragile girl who's suffered an attack. But Violet's true self shines through her wild, black eyes. She's dead of emotion, a tangle of rage and brutality.

And terrifying.

As Violet stands, focus switched to me, Maxwell calls out, and the bear charges forward towards the balcony, where he'll easily jump down and escape.

Only the bear doesn't jump.

Both paws slam into Violet's chest, taking her by surprise before she can retaliate. The wooden balcony rail behind her splinters with the force only two supernaturals could cause, and Violet screams out her fury as she falls backwards over the edge.

In the following seconds, I eye the bear, who's now focused on me, as I wait for Violet to scale the house and reach the balcony again.

Maxwell commands his pet to hold off. The bear doesn't move, head now bowed, injured but not incapacitated despite the amount of blood flowing—how long would his shifter strength have endured Violet's attack?

Nothing happens.

The witch doesn't speak.

I'm rooted with indecision.

In the silence, smoke drifts further up the stairs, now framing Maxwell with a hazy cloud.

"Oh dear," he whispers.

Outside, an anguished scream unlike anything I've heard in my life echoes through my soul, biting through to the marrow of my bones. Then another, only this time, a word that changes my life forever.

"Violet!"

Violet. I rush blindly to the balcony.

No.

And rather than running like someone with sense would, the gloating, murderous witch joins me and stands close to an enemy blinded with wrath.

If I hadn't looked over the broken balcony, would I have paused for thought?

If I'd paused when I saw Violet, unmoving, with the fence post protruding from her chest, would I have told myself she isn't dead?

If the girl who holds my heart in her hands didn't have hers impaled, would I have chosen a different future?

Because the glee on Maxwell's face seals his fate and mine.

I punch a fist into the witch's chest and tear out the bastard's heart.

Chapter Thirty-Four

VIOLET

Voices around filter into my dreams, urgent, panicked, yelling. Something about Kai unconscious and locked in a boat shed. A bear in the woods. A loud argument about a witch.

But my dreams have no images, and an agonizing pain spreads through me, worse than any I could imagine, having never suffered from the misfortune.

I'm not dreaming.

Rowan's close by, his magic screaming as loud as his voice, Leif urging him to focus. Somebody cradles my head, his blood yanking me from consciousness to acute awareness that I am not asleep.

My eyes struggle open, white spots dancing before them, and I gasp in a huge breath, lungs filling with welcome air. If I had the energy, I'd seize the arm holding me and take the blood beckoning from Grayson's veins. Instead, another set of hands pulls me from Grayson, and I'm dragged into an embrace I can't return as the person sits on the ground holding me.

The movement twists pain into my heart, and I take a sharp breath before looking down at the bloodied wound in my chest. The last moments of consciousness zip across my mind, those seconds after the post pierced my chest. Not fear. Only a single question.

And to find the answer, I had to die.

Looks like I won the battle I had with the tall fence post.

"Violet." I focus on Rowan's gray face, looking down at me. His wet hair touches my face as his hands cover my cheeks, and he kisses my forehead, squeezing me until I wince.

I'm on damp ground, a short distance from the lodge, where the front's damaged by blackened wood and smashed windows. All three guys surround me and the faint scent from a dying fire fills my nostrils, joined by the earthy smell I love that comes after the rain.

"You died," Rowan mumbles against my forehead. "Your heart stopped. Ten minutes. Thought I'd lost you."

"Then evidently I *am* immortal," I reply, barely recognizing my weak voice. "How fortunate."

"And unfortunately, Maxwell was *not* immortal," says Leif tersely. "What the fuck do we do now?"

Past tense.

I struggle to sit. How long does post-death weakness last? Because although grateful for the immortality, I'm unimpressed by my limbs' refusal to co-operate.

"Grayson!" snaps Leif. "Tell Violet."

Grayson now stands further away from me, staring at the lake as if he isn't quite with the world. He pulls something from his jacket pocket and drops it onto the muddy ground at his feet. My eyes aren't working correctly, and I focus harder.

A heart.

I stare at the bloodied hand dangling by his side. "Good grief, Grayson. What have you done?"

To Be Continued in Thornwood Academy 3: For Dear Life available summer 2023

OTHER BOOKS BY LJ SWALLOW

Nightworld Academy
Reverse Harem YA Paranormal series
Term One
Term Two
Term Three
Term Four
Term Five
Term Six
Also available as two box sets
Connected Books
Winterfall Magic
Winterfall Witch
Blackwood Magic

Ravenhold Supernatural Reform Academy
Reverse Harem Dark Academy
Witch Born
Magic Forged
Blood Legacy
Available as a box set

The Four Horsemen Series
Reverse Harem Urban Fantasy
Legacy
Bound
Hunted
Guardians
Chaos
Descent
Reckoning
or as two box sets

Printed in Great Britain
by Amazon

30901411R00131